I0724210

WILDFIRE

MIDNIGHT SUN 3

LYNN BURKE

Copyright © 2021 by Lynn Burke

All rights reserved.

Editor: Avril Stepowski

Cover Art by Golden Czermak / FuriousFotog

This is a work of fiction. Names, characters, places, and incidents are the product of the author's imagination or are used fictitiously, and any resemblance to actual persons, living or dead, business establishments, events, or locales is entirely coincidental.

No part of this book may be reproduced in any form, except for the inclusion of brief quotations in a review or article, without written permission from the author.

Visit my website at authorlynnburke.com

WILDFIRE

A child born of the wilderness, I don't know many women. Never had one of my own.

But sassy little Annie Charran owned my heart long before I stole her first kiss. She paid a high price for my actions, and even though I want her for life, I'll never fit into the one she has planned for herself.

Given the opportunity to beg forgiveness, I grab it—and end up facing death.

With instincts overriding my senses, I take again.

But this time, a wildfire flares, demolishing everything in its path. Survival means sacrifice, and for me, life trumps dreams.

I'll force Annie to give up what she wants most, even if it means I lose her forever.

1

ANNIE

"What will you do if he happens to stop by?" Mom's voice, muffled by the headset, reached me over the plane's rumbling engine as she flew us deep into the wilderness.

I stared at the snow-capped mountains to my right, knowing who she spoke of, but I didn't have a ready answer. "Not sure," I stated the truth. Part of me longed to see his face after eight years, the other part of me wanted to scar up that face for what he'd put me through.

The first time I saw him, I fell in love. Only twelve years old, a little girl whose hormones had yet to kick in and put me on the right path like the rest of my friends, and I'd got warm fuzzies in my belly over his lopsided smirk. Imagined hearts in my eyes like those silly old-time cartoons I sometimes caught Mom and Dad watching.

Young love…it set me to dreaming of having what my parents did after twenty something years together. Unconditional. Affection all the time. Mad love, the type that made Dad act like a bear sometimes in defending Mom or when looking out for her.

I wanted a man like my dad. He always claimed he'd "grown up" in the wilds of Alaska even though he hadn't moved there until later in life, but I knew such a one. A young man who had grown up out in the middle of nowhere and seemed the sort to turn into an animal in order to protect his loved ones.

Roan Kelly.

It'd been eight years since he'd stolen my first kiss, eight years since he'd burned me—literally—and broke my heart by not seeming to care.

He'd come to town once a few years back, but I made sure to be *out* of town at my cousin Kari's house in Fairbanks. I didn't want to see him, didn't want to get caught up in those green eyes of his that seemed to read clear through to my soul and sent shivers from head to toes.

Last I'd seen him had been when Dad carried me toward the plane Mom had fired to life, the searing pain in my hand stealing my breath and sending tears down my cheeks. Roan hadn't followed on our heels like a man sorry for what he'd done. He didn't ask forgiveness, didn't apologize for being the one who'd caused me serious injury and the possibility of ending my dreams. He'd stayed right where we left him—by the fire pit, hands fisted at his sides. Mute and emotionless.

He'd gotten what he'd wanted—my first kiss—and obviously didn't care enough about me to make sure I was okay.

I hadn't been for a very long time.

I glanced down at my hands clasped lightly on my lap. My right still had ragged, ugly as sin scars on some fingers. I didn't release my hold to inspect the palm. Those scars remained, too. Even after grafts, evidence of falling hands first into a burned down bonfire full of glowing, red-hot coals couldn't be erased, nor could the phantom pain that lingered. A constant reminder I couldn't get rid of.

If he hadn't caught me the first time, stolen my sweet sixteen a day early, chased after me when I'd sprinted off full of giddiness and elation at his fulfilling my secret fantasy I would never verbally admit to…

But years later, I'd found another perfect man who sent similar shivers to my toes—until he, too, broke my heart. The pain of that lingered as well, but for a whole different reason.

Letting out a sigh, I turned my focus on the window beside me, staring out over the Alaskan wilderness far below Mom's old plane she refused to retire.

The thing was old as shit, but still ran like a dream. The first Midnight Sun Charter plane, her precious '54 Beaver. Mom and Dad's business had grown over the years. Five other planes, two of which ran joy rides for paying vacationers wanting to experience Alaska from the skies.

I'd co-piloted with Dad a few times, and it's where I'd met the second love of my life as we'd flown his family to see the sights. He hadn't looked anything like Roan. Didn't have the same deep voice, the dark hair, and vibrant green eyes, but my heart ended up broken regardless.

Different men. Same result.

I'm not made for that kind of love.

That truth had run countless times in my head, but at least my heart didn't ache as bad as it had a month earlier.

"You okay, sweetie?"

I turned toward Mom, hearing the clear concern in her voice muffled through the headset, and forced a smile. "Yeah."

"You're sure about this?"

Rolling my eyes, I snorted a huff.

"I know, I know," she said with a sigh, turning once more to look out the plane's windshield. "You've assured me a million times over this is what you want."

"Yeah." I, too, looked ahead, waiting for the turn that would bring our homestead into view. "It's just a broken heart, Mom. I'm not some damsel in distress hoping to find my knight in shining armor out in the woods."

"It could happen," she said with a shrug and smirk.

Yeah, it had happened for her, but if nothing else, my ex tackled those daydreams to the ground.

"Love will come when you aren't looking for it."

"With what?" I motioned toward the vast nothingness out the windows. "A griz? A wolf?"

Mom didn't laugh. "You carry that pistol, knife, and sat phone everywhere you go, understood?"

"Yes, *Dad*." Sarcasm oozed, but he'd said the same thing a dozen times before seeing us off.

"He's not any happier than I am about this, but I'd rather have you be a forty-minute flight away than overseas like you considered doing when Justin… Sorry."

Yeah, the dreamer in me thought. *Head to Tuscany and forget all about my ex.*

"It's okay, Mom," I murmured.

I'd considered falling for an Italian who owned an olive orchard but only because I loved olives, not because I was interested in allowing myself to be vulnerable ever again. A case of olives packed in the cargo area behind us. They would be the love of my life.

"I'm going to be just fine."

"I know, sweetie. You're one of the strongest young women I know."

"And the summers at the homestead prepared me for the zombie apocalypse," I reminded her with a small laugh, knowing it to be the absolute damn truth. "I got this."

Mom smiled and reached over to squeeze my hand. "You

get bored or lonely, I'll come for a visit. Girls weekend. Wine, chocolate, and sleeping in."

While that sounded like a lot of fun, I wanted quiet time to finish writing the three-book series I'd been working on for what seemed like forever. It didn't help that I had put my dreams of becoming a published author aside for my ex—because my daydreaming and writing took too much time away from him.

Insecure bastard.

He'd demanded all my attention, and I'd given it to him because I'd been so desperate to find what my parents had. I had come to realize the truth of that fact—and his damn insecurities—but had been blinded for too long by the warm fuzzies. By hope. By dreams. With my second broken heart, that whole twenty-twenty hindsight shit hit hard.

Dad was one of a kind and growing up in our household had instilled unrealistic expectations in my heart. I'd never find someone who looked at me like I supplied their oxygen—but holy hell, I still wanted it. Dreamed of it. Scribbled stories in my journals since childhood about fairy lands, trolls, and elves. True love fated by cupid's arrow.

It's time to put me first, just like Mom always told me to do.

"I won't be a pushover ever again," I murmured half to myself, thinking about the choice I'd finally made for *me*.

"Good," Mom snipped the word in my headset. "I never liked how you gave up yourself for Justin."

I lifted my chin. "I'm back to good old bitch Annie—selfish and independent. A woman who refuses to settle."

"That's my girl." Mom laughed while banking toward the south. "You make me proud."

The Charran homestead appeared in the distance, the small one-room cabin's gray logs nearly blending into the brush along the river. Dad had ripped off the roof and built up the walls higher to put in a loft above their bed for Junior and me, but other than that, the cabin looked the same since I could remember seeing it the first time at three years of age.

Dad had shown Junior and me how to survive in the wilderness, how to hunt, fish, and track. Every summer, our family filled my mind up with memories, and I, in turn, filled up countless journals with stories long lost.

Once upon a time, the homestead had been what I'd looked forward to the most. Quiet to write. Quality time with loved ones. An occasional visit from Roan and his family who lived upriver. Until that fateful night all those years ago when I learned he'd only wanted a kiss and couldn't be bothered to worry about the injury he'd caused.

Men and their damn selfish desires.

I let out another sigh, knowing Mom would head to the Kelly homestead next with the pile of spring supplies behind mine, but I didn't mention their son's name, nor did I want to talk or think about him.

He'd broken my heart first, brought on that first inkling of mistrusting love. My ex, Justin, just hammered the truth home.

Two men. Two broken hearts.

I'm so done. It's me time, bitch.

Smirking at the fact I spoke to my muse with excitement for the first time in years, I looked forward to settling in. Pouring myself some wine, curling up by the fire, and typing away.

No internet, no social media to distract me. No man sneering or laughing at my "unattainable" dreams.

I would have my three-book series hammered out in a matter of months. Three before I had any plans of company—

no matter how much mom called the sat phone and bugged me to let her visit.

Dad sat at home recovering from having his appendix taken out, and Junior went and got himself hitched a few years back, his wife popping out two boys who looked just like him in two years. She hated the homestead, and he loved her like Mom did Dad.

So, no Junior. No Dad—and no Mom.

Just me and you.

I imagined my muse laughed maniacally in my head, rubbing her hands together with glee.

Time for *us*, time for taking control over my life and fulfilling my dream, one I would let no man take from me ever again.

ROAN

I cast into the river below Pa's cabin, the plop of my lure lost in the noise of water finding its way between rocks and boulders. Fish weren't biting, but I hadn't been intent on catching anything for dinner, anyway. My gaze strayed to the east more often than it did across the water looking for better places to fish.

The waiting, I hated—but I no longer held my breath in anticipation.

After eight years, I gave up hoping Annie would be in the cockpit with her mom or dad when they flew supplies in. Didn't keep my heart from thumping heavily every time my ears caught the drone of a plane engine approaching. I made sure to be around the homestead on delivery days…just in case.

The real reason for my fishing rather than out hiking in peace and quiet.

Far as I knew, Annie hadn't ever forgiven me for kissing her without consent on the night before her sixteenth birthday, then being the one responsible for her burned hand. All because I'd wanted another taste of her soft lips and sweet breath and had chased her around the dying fire after her parents had retired to their tent and Ma and Pa to our cabin.

The guilt, my inability to react to her pain, embarrassed the hell out of me. I never spoke of it, never admitted to my parents what I'd done, *why* she'd been running and fell into the fire.

Because I'd become an animal acting on selfish instincts alone. Salivating at her heels like a starved wolf. My lack of control had caused the one woman I wanted to leave our homestead in a rushed escape by plane.

Her dad had returned a few days later for their belongings, but even then, I'd hightailed it to the hills to keep from having to face him, his anger, for causing his little girl pain. It wasn't until a year later that I'd learned through Ma that Annie had healed up enough to have full use of her hand.

I still dreamed of her, waking at least once a week with my cock a single stroke away from erupting in spurts of sticky white. Damned instincts.

She'd been my first kiss.

My only kiss.

And at fuckin' twenty-seven, I felt doomed to a solitary life, never knowing what it felt like to lose myself between a woman's thighs. Brock had taken me to town with Pa's blessing when I'd turned twenty-one to open a savings account of my own for my share of skins and gold we panned together. Brock had offered his home for a short time, to enjoy the sights of the town, perhaps find a woman— same as Pa had suggested.

But I'd fled back to the wilderness rather than take advantage of the Charran's hospitality.

Too much noise.

Too many lights.

Unbearable smells.

And no woman I'd seen compared to the dark-haired beauty who'd stolen my heart when I'd been nothing but a kid. Annie had made herself scarce that single day I'd been in town. Didn't catch one glimpse of her.

Little Annie Charran.

I cast again, teeth clenched against a groan as my cock stirred in my pants, same as every time I thought too long on her.

Spitfire with the kind of life in her dark eyes that sets a man's soul on fire. The kind of smile and laughter that makes life worth living.

Until you take away that smile, that laughter.

Jessie told me her daughter had healed up just fine the first time I'd found the balls to face one of her parents after the accident. Brock had assured me there was no ill will with the following delivery, but their family never flew out to visit again the way they'd used to.

And the Kelly family never hiked down river to visit during the summer months, either.

Time dragged on while I waited on the plane every spring and fall, only to be disappointed again to find the co-pilot seat empty. Brock and Jessie had forgiven me once I'd manned up and asked for it without going into details of what had truly happened. And I'd heard through Ma who heard from Jessie over a sat phone call once, that Annie didn't want an apology. Wouldn't offer forgiveness no matter how much I groveled.

Sassy, stubborn girl, but that part of her made me hard, too.

Pa suggested a mail order bride when I got too cranky and restless, and as the years slipped by and the woman who'd burrowed into my head never showed, I began to give his suggestion some thought.

"Need a cabin and land first, though," I muttered my usual excuse to myself while reeling in my lure.

Ma and Pa offered a parcel of their acreage up past the berry brambles, but I wanted a bit of distance, even if I couldn't afford it. Couldn't have my sisters stopping by whenever they felt the need to drive me insane.

But did I want a woman I'd never met? Was it possible a woman existed with more beauty, more fire, than my Annie?

My much younger twin sisters teased me that I'd lost my heart to her because she's the only woman outside them, Ma, and Jessie I'd ever met.

But I'd seen dozens of women in town.

And my heart knew, just like Pa told me his did when he'd first seen Ma. She was life, and mine turned up empty every fuckin' day without her.

Tired of casting, I set aside my pole and scoured the area for spiders a ways from the river's edge before settling onto my ass. Cotton grass rose around me, their seed heads waving in the gentle breeze ruffling my too-long hair Ma needed to cut. The lichen beneath my backside had all but dried out since we'd had less snow than normal that winter, and the spring hadn't brought much-needed rain.

The land around me appeared as bleak as my hopes for *more* even though Mother Nature's time of renewal had come.

A low hum I recognized ticked my heart rate up—but it approached from down river.

Brow furrowing, I stood, scanning the blue sky to the east thinking my ears deceived me. The hum grew louder to my right, and I angled that way. Less than a minute later, Jessie's plane appeared.

I grabbed up my pole and hiked through the grass tussocks, taking care to keep from their clumps so as not to roll an ankle as I'd done dozens of times in my childhood before learning better. The plane buzzed up behind me, flew overhead, and I tilted my chin high, adrenaline rushing to thump my heart as it always did when Jessie's old plane flew over our home.

She banked and descended low enough I could make her out in the cockpit as she readied to land on the river.

Alone.

No Annie.

Hating the feeling of my heart falling yet again even though I'd felt sure I hadn't put any hope in seeing her, I slowed my steps. No sense rushing to unload supplies and having to carry the bulk of them up to the cabin. Ciarra and Nissa, my sisters, would help, as would Ma, but Pa and I would see to most of the work— same as always.

Both girls squealed as Jessie's pontoons dragged in the water, their giggles and excitement while rushing down the path to the river lifting my lips. I expected they looked forward to the bags of books Jessie always brought from the library's yearly spring clean out—same as me.

Ma had taught us to read, and I devoured everything dropped off at our place. Thrillers, mysteries, romance…I loved them all. Even though I had no wish to live elsewhere, or even visit for that matter, I sure as hell enjoyed reading about it. Living vicariously through an author's imagination.

Jessie hopped out of the cockpit, tied up to the log ramp Pa and I had replaced a week earlier, and she hugged both my sisters, their words lost in the breeze blowing in my face.

Ma and Pa approached at a slower pace, holding hands as usual when making their way down the pebbled path, but Jessie's smile my way took the sting of longing for a similar relationship away. I felt my own grin grow.

A visitor, even if only for a short time, brought much needed excitement to the wilderness.

Jessie eyed my beard I'd let grow out over the winter, her smirk and the light in her eyes letting me know she approved of how I'd let myself go. "Looking good, kid!" she called my way.

I set aside my pole and accepted the hug she offered, her scent sweet as vanilla.

Pa and Ma came up behind me, and more hugs, more words of welcome took a few minutes like it always did.

"No Brock or Annie," Ma mentioned—for my benefit in hoping for word of her, I expected.

"Brock had emergency surgery two days ago."

"What happened?" Pa asked before I could question Jessie.

"Appendix."

"He okay?" I asked.

"He's fine." Jessie nodded toward the plane with her head, her way of telling us it was time to unload so she could get back to him. "Annie's down at the homestead."

My feet stayed planted, heart stuttered out, and kicked back to life as my family fell into line behind her. "Alone?"

"Yeah." Jessie pulled open the plane's side door and climbed inside. "She said she's needing some peace and quiet to find herself."

"If any woman besides you and Saige can make it out here alone, it's Annie." Pa took the first box while Jessie beamed over his words of praise.

"She's a strong one," Jessie agreed, turning to take up another box and hand them off to my waiting sisters and Ma. They exchanged a few words, but my brain buzzed.

Annie.

A two days' walk away.

Alone.

Vulnerable—no, scratch that. The woman was anything but vulnerable. Even at a day shy of sixteen, last I'd seen her, she'd been a feisty one. The kind that would face a grizzly like her dad had done and live to tell about it.

Pa and the women headed up the pebbled path, and I reached for the box Jessie held out to me.

"Do me a favor, Roan?" she asked, still grasping the box so I couldn't turn away.

"Whatever you need." I meant the words, too.

"Would you check on her in a couple weeks? Make sure she's doing okay? She's a strong woman, but she's also stubborn as hell."

"She'll stay down there no matter what she encounters," I added, knowing exactly what Jessie had meant.

She smiled and released the box with a wink. "Seems you know my daughter."

I did. We'd been damn near inseparable throughout our teenage years.

"She'd like to see you," Jessie stated quietly, keeping my feet firmly planted in place with her steady gaze.

"I doubt that," I muttered, reminded yet again of that phone conversation between her and Ma that had damn near broken me.

"I caught her looking upriver more than once while we unpacked her things."

I wasn't one to keep from sharing the truth—except for the time I'd turned into an animal. But maybe it was time for honesty. Maybe voicing my embarrassment, my unrelenting guilt would make things better.

"I was chasing her that night," I admitted after a quick glance up the path to make sure my family wasn't close by. "I stole her sweet sixteen from her, lost my head, and became nothing more than a drooling dog."

"She told me."

I jerked my focus back toward Jessie to find a small smile still on her lips. "She did?"

"Girls like to gossip."

"I feel like shit for what I did—sorry for cursing, ma'am," I muttered.

"And I feel like a *shitty* mom for not being able to get through her thick skull that you hadn't meant to cause her any harm."

My lips twitched. Annie sure got her sassiness from her mom. "I stood there and stared. Couldn't move, couldn't think. Nothing but a damn chickenshit."

"It's called shock," Jessie stated firmly, "and it's not unusual, nor is it ever too late to ask for forgiveness—in person."

Pa started back down the path.

"I'll never be good enough for Annie, even if she does find it in her heart to forgive me." I kept my voice low. "She's a goshawk and I'm a chickadee. She could rule the skies if she wanted—and she needs and deserves a better man by her side through life."

"Roan."

"Yes, ma'am?" I tore my focus off the box of canned peaches I'd taken to staring at, not sure if it was the thought of sweet fruit or Annie that set my mouth to drooling.

She smiled at me. "What she *needs* is a man who is going to support her. Her dreams. Her wants in life."

I nodded even though I didn't understand why she told me what Annie needed. I couldn't support myself, my *own* dreams, let alone someone else's.

"Yes, ma'am, she does." Turning away, my heart fell a

little bit more. So much for making things better by spilling my guts.

I'd heard Annie didn't want an apology, and knowing her sassy ass, that meant she never wanted to lay eyes on me again, but I'd made a promise to her Ma. If nothing else, I was a man of my word.

I would stop by to check in on Jessie's daughter.

My cock twitched at the thought of filling my eyes with Annie again, but I grit my teeth and strode up toward the cabin, reminding myself there was no point in hoping I'd get even a portion of what I wanted from her—not even forgiveness.

Given that littlest bit, I felt maybe I could find some sort of contentment in my life.

But I doubted she'd let go of her stubborn self, no matter how much I begged.

3

———

ANNIE

I'd gotten over my fear of fire for the most part. Enough I could light kindling and cook over an open flame again. I just took my time and extra care and wore oven mitts when getting anywhere near a hot pot. I also never threw plastic into the fire like Junior had done that night, leaving a glob of melted shit that had stuck to my hand—almost *ruined* my hand.

Twisting off the cap of one of the small bottles of wine I'd brought along, I ambled toward the recliner Dad had brought to the homestead the summer before. Old bones and all that shit, he'd complained even though the man could still work the homestead like a twenty-something guy.

A perfect chair to sit in, prop my feet up, and open my MacBook before darkness took over the sky.

The cabin's interior had changed a bit over the years. A bigger table, Pa's special chair being the larger additions. A couple pictures hung on the walls where tools and shelves didn't clutter. A new mantle spanned over the fireplace and Pa's newer battery storage packs filled by solar panels sat tucked away in the far corner.

17

I didn't understand exactly how they worked, but I knew how to keep my computer, sat phone, and rechargeable flashlights and lamps full and ready for use. An old oil lamp still sat in the table's center, though, just in case, and another on Ma and Pa's bed stand.

While Ma would have unpacked the boxes of supplies I'd brought along, stocking them on the kitchen shelves and beneath their bed in the rollaway drawers, I left them stacked behind the door.

I had better things to do. Dive into my writing and leave the world behind every second I could for the next couple of months.

I got lost, my fingers flying over the keys, my emotions swept up along in the ride I'd plotted out and the world I'd created. The characters who'd been whispering through my muse for years, awaiting their time and my attention began to clamber once more for my focus, and I gave it to them fully.

My eyes burned as I whispered back an apology in my mind while cracking open the second single serve bottle of wine.

Never again, I promised them, swigging straight from the plastic bottle.

More words flew from my fingertips. More wine poured down my throat.

Darkness descended, and I turned on the battery-operated lamp on the small table beside me, settling in again for another one thousand words in the following hour. My characters had been flirting on the edge of passion set aside for years, and I finally had the chance to bring all their desires to fruition.

I expected my heart rate to rise along with hers as he finally cradled her face in his hands, his lips tasting hers.

Where warmth should have grown between my thighs

over their slowly undressing one another, his gentle caresses along her bared body, I sat unmoved.

Almost bored.

Frowning, I relaxed back into my chair, staring at the words on my screen.

Their supposed passion that had been pent up and ready to explode sure as hell wasn't *exploding*. It needed…more.

Closing my eyes, I tipped my head back and emptied my head of the scene I'd planned, how I thought I'd wanted it to unfold to readers. Instead, I put myself into the story rather than watching like a fly on the wall.

What would I want if I was her?

What would I want him to do?

How would I want him to touch me? Kiss me?

While my ex hadn't ever been anything but gentle, hindsight made me aware of just how selfish a lover he'd been. Not that I had anything to compare him to. He'd been the only man to get me into bed.

Roan was the only other man I'd kissed—and he'd taken. Without apology, the memory of his hard kiss, his hungry tongue, teeth, and lips eating at my mouth as though trying to devour my soul…

Lust, hot and wet, rose as it did every time I relived our single kiss, and I shifted on the chair.

My back against a tree. His hands fisted in my long hair. Hard muscle and scraping scruff of a nineteen-year-old man who hadn't shaved for three days had set my entire body on fire.

Eyelids popping open, I leaned forward, fingers on the keys, deleting out the entire scene I'd forced, and started again, allowing the fantasy in my mind to unfold.

My hero *took*. Unapologetic in his frantic need to finally have what he'd been craving for months. He devoured her mouth like a man long denied sustenance. Air. Food. *Life*. And she fought back, but only in urgent desire to do the same, trying to touch every inch of his skin when he trapped her hands overhead. She soaked in his groans over her taste, melted beneath his roughened palms, his bruising fingertips.

Rising emotions damn near choked me as my fingers flew, fast as my heartbeat.

Coming together.

Dirty words. Frantic thrusts.

Yes. Hell, yes.

Grinning, and with a bit of buzzed giggling, I brought them to completion. The big O, reached at the same time—a necessity, and something else I'd never experienced. He'd done it for her, though, the grinding of his pelvis on her clit enough to send her tumbling into the most mind-blowing orgasm she'd ever known.

Leaking a slow breath between my lips, I sat back, my heart still thumping, the arousal in me far from sated like the characters on my screen.

"Damnit." I set aside my computer and rubbed a hand down over my throbbing core. Panties and leggings soaked clear through met my fingertips. A few flicks to my clit would bring relief, but I wanted more.

A rubber dick would have to do since I had no man—and no plans of letting another one touch me anytime soon.

I hopped up and dug through my bathroom bin at the foot of the bed until I found my toys. A quick scramble to rid my lower half of clothing, and I laid back on the bed, sinking the dildo deep into my sopping mess.

"Holy hell." I tipped up my hips to take it deeper, eyes closing to relive the scene I'd written—but with me as the female lead. I teased myself with slow drags in and out, the rubber quickly warming, but harder than the real thing. More *filling*.

I imagined his kiss. His hands running over the swell of my small breasts, to the swollen nub, and wetness below. It was his fingers running alongside my throbbing clit. His thumb that finally swept over it and down, the upward rub jerking my hips up off the bed.

Lower lip between my teeth, I teased myself, his dirty words of how much he wanted to fill me with his cum while thrusting into me tingling my climax up from my toes.

The lover my imagination swelled to life was no CPA like my ex. His hands weren't smooth from working at a desk all day, his cheeks clean shaven. Seasoned, roughened hands took what they wanted from my willing body, scruff scraping my skin, teeth and suction of his mouth bruising my body—

"Roan…" I groaned his name as my insides clenched down on rubber, wetness swelling with every orgasmic contraction around it.

Roan.

"Holy hell." The involuntary twitches ended, and I stilled, the dildo still shoved deep inside my body, my other arm thrown over my face as I sucked down oxygen.

Why? Why did I have to go and put a face and name to the fantasy?

Scowling, I pulled the dildo from the tight grip of my pussy and sat up. I'd creamed all over the damn thing, even made a mess on the sheet beneath me.

"Fuck." I tossed aside the dildo, hating the fact I would have to do a load of laundry long before I'd planned on it.

One negative about living off grid. Good old wash bucket and hand wringing.

"No more getting myself off," I grumbled to myself while cleaning up. Once I righted my lower half with clothing, washed up my used toy, and shoved it back in the bottom of the bin, I returned to my chair.

But the words wouldn't come.

I sucked down the rest of my last little bottle in the 4-pack and crawled into bed. Sunrise would bring a new day, another new beginning. Closing my eyes, I worked through the next scene, hating it fell flat from the fantasies still lingering in my mind and tingling my body.

Cursing, I rolled. Punched my pillow and buried my face in it.

Sleep became the bitch, denying me what I wanted.

4

ROAN

"Where are you headed?"

I shoved an extra shirt into my backpack. "To check on Annie."

Ma didn't reply right away, and I finished packing enough things to see me through for at least a week. Plenty of time to hike down river, do as I'd promised Jessie, and return home.

Heart guarded up tight against the only woman I wanted.

A friendly neighborly visit—if she didn't peer down the length of a shotgun barrel the second I stepped onto Charran property.

"Are you sure that's a good idea?"

I zipped my backpack and turned to find Ma studying my face, concern in her eyes.

"She broke your heart all those years ago," she continued when I didn't answer, "and if I'm being honest, you haven't been the same since."

Being honest... Maybe telling *Ma* the truth might help ease the ache in my heart and the guilt eating at my guts.

"There's more to the story, Ma," I mumbled, unable to meet her gaze.

She waited—so I continued. I'd taken without asking. Chased her for more, Junior's laughter egging me on. Her falling into the red embers, screaming, and jumping up, a glob of what I learned later was melted plastic stuck to her hand.

The pain in her cries, the tears, the accusing glances she'd tossed my way as her father carried her off. The sure hatred in a gaze I couldn't hold—both Annie's *and* Junior's even if he had laughed at my determination to get my hands on his little sister.

I'd choked on the horror of what I'd done. And I hadn't woken from my stupor to beg forgiveness until the Charran family flew off into the night.

"I learned some hard lessons that night, Ma."

She clasped my scruffy cheeks in her tiny hands, drawing my attention to her big brown eyes. Pa had said she'd been shy as anything when they'd first met, hardly looking him in the face, but Ma had learned some hard lessons, too. Ones neither parent shied away from telling me and my sisters.

Grandpa had gone off hunting and never returned, leaving his young, abused wife to find comfort in the man dying to give it to her. I'd been born nine and a half months later, but my parentage hadn't ever been questioned. I had Flynn Kelly's green eyes—from his mother's side. The only blood belonging to Grandpa Callan running through my veins had come directly through his son, my Pa.

A kind-hearted man who never raised a hand to any of us kids or Ma. A man more rugged than the hills around us, more instinctual a protective parent than any momma grizzly.

"Accidents happen."

While I knew that to be true, the life-altering accident had a cause—me. "I lost control, Ma."

"And you learned your lesson."

"That's not the point."

"I think it is, son," Ma argued, still holding my face, and staring up at me. "And you need to forgive yourself for what you did before you go traipsing off with a fragile heart, hinging the rest of your life on a stubborn girl accepting your apology. She hasn't wanted it up to this point, why cause yourself more heartache?"

"Because I promised Jessie I'd check in on her, and if nothing else, I'm going to be a man of my word."

"You *are* a good man, Roan Kelly," Ma said, her voice low and tight as though she fought off tears. "And don't you go forgetting it, either. Any woman would be lucky to have you as a partner in life."

Maybe one who wanted the same kind of life I did— secluded from society. Quiet and peaceful. Not a woman who'd grown up with all the fancy frills I'd seen firsthand, all the gadgets and electricity that comes with living in town.

A mail-order bride looking for just that would be my best bet.

Certainly not little Annie Charran who'd had nothing but privilege her whole life—never mind her hatred for me.

"Thanks, Ma," I whispered, leaning down to kiss her forehead.

She smiled and patted my cheek. "Let me pack you some food for the hike."

Both of my sisters scampered over to me when I exited the cabin a short time later, eyeing the backpack strapped to my shoulder and the rifle in my hand.

"Where are you going?" Ciarra asked while Nissa grumbled about all the freedom Pa allowed me.

"Down river."

Nissa's muttering cut off, a twinkle lighting her dark eyes. "Off to claim yourself a bride?"

"Shut up, Nis." I started off, turning my focus southward.

"Roan and Annie, up in a tree," Ciarra sang with a giggle, Nissa joining her in on the next part while I scowled and cursed Junior for teaching them that damn, silly song all those years ago.

At almost eighteen, they knew nothing about that night and should have been a little more mature rather than skipping after me. Both longed to go to town and see everything Ma had told us about, everything I'd grumbled over when they'd sat me down and hounded me for every bit of information they could when I'd returned home my one time out of the wilderness. Pa had promised both they'd get there some day come hell or high water.

I knew neither would return. They would find their happily-ever-afters like all their favorite characters in the romance books they devoured within days of Jessie bringing them to us. Ma had found hers in the wilderness, but my fanciful sisters didn't have the same makeup as Ma. They both had boundless energy and life inside them—same as Annie.

She hadn't returned except for some quiet time from what Jessie had said, and I knew my sisters wouldn't either.

———

Long-dried grasses made up a soft bed beneath me, ones I'd checked good and careful for spiders before bedding down, and I stared up at the expanse of stars overhead, the occasional crackle from the small fire at my side the only noise in the night. I remembered the racket of town, and again counted myself lucky, blessed, to be able to bed down in complete, peaceful silence. No obnoxious horns beeping. No thumping music as cars drove past.

Not even Pa's light snores or Nissa's answering ones.

Grinning, I clasped my hands atop my stomach filled with one of the sandwiches Ma had packed for me.

This is living.

My smile faded, though, as I considered the solitary life I'd chosen to that point. Would it be more fulfilling having someone with me? Even if no passion, no lust ever rose between us like I'd felt with Annie? Would I be more comfortable having an extra set of hands, an ear to listen, a warm body in bed with mine during the long, cold nights?

I imagined such a life with Annie and scowled over my dick's immediate response.

"Fuckin' hell," I groaned, grasping my hard length through my pants. No way I could show up at the Charran homestead with a load brewing in my balls. She'd meet me with a shotgun for sure. Maybe if I emptied them enough while traveling there, I'd be thoroughly spent and in absolute control once I saw her again.

Hell knew, the sixteen-year-old Annie had messed with my head to the point I'd become more animal than man. Twenty-four-year-old Annie? A full-grown woman with the same sparkling eyes and sassy mouth?

Fuck.

I yanked open my pants and palmed my length, slickening my hand up good with the pre-cum oozing from its tip.

I cursed through grit teeth, my hips thrusting my aching dick through my wet grip. "Fuck." I lifted my head off the ground and watched the head of my dick disappear between my fingers, and reappear on downward strokes, the wet schlicking sounds tightening my balls up against my body.

The first shot of cum ribboned into the air, still falling toward my stomach when the second spurt erupted.

I made a fuckin' mess, cleaned up with clumps of dried grass, and finally closed my eyes.

Sated. For the time being.

In the morning, I emptied my balls again before starting off. Again when I stopped for lunch, and once more before bedding down for my second night beneath the stars. A bit chaffed from all the attention, I let it go the next morning.

By afternoon, I knew I drew close since I'd cut across land rather than stick to the river's edge. The second I caught sight of smoke curling into the sky, I paused, hands beneath my backpack straps on my shoulders, and watched the black dissipate into the cloudless blue above.

Over the rise. Less than a mile.

My chest felt tight, like a log pressed against me, pushing me into the earth, and I parted my lips to better breathe oxygen into my lungs. Although I sweated from the hike, a shiver raised the hairs on my arms and neck.

Excitement coiled in my stomach. Swelled my dick.

Need launched my feet forward, my stride eating up the space between me and the woman drawing me in like she'd cast and sunk her hook deep in my throat. Reeling me in. Faster, racing my heart.

Would she rip out the hook and leave me floundering? Or would she be gentle in its removal, eventually sending me back the way I'd come, allowing me to live?

Don't want to live without her.

The thought shot through my brain, solidifying in my heart, no matter how much I lacked. She wouldn't ever have me, but perhaps I *could* find a way to mend the hurt between us.

It would have to be enough.

Jaw clenched and gaze set on the cabin that came into sight as I topped the rise, I told myself I was a man in control. Nothing would hinder me from making things right. I wouldn't take—I would give until she caved and accepted my apology.

I also refused to hope for more.

5

ANNIE

I sat in the outhouse taking care of business, staring at the dried pine boards making up the door two feet from my face.

Ten days at the homestead, and I'd already written close to fifty-thousand words. Just over half-way through book one of three I planned to complete. I was well on my way and enjoying the quiet, eating whenever I wanted, on no one's schedule but my own.

Drinking a pot of coffee throughout the morning helped wake me, hiking in the afternoon refreshed my mind, and settling in with my computer after dinner again gave me a sense of accomplishment before the daylight hours even ended.

A stir-fry of canned chicken, peas, and rice sat on the back of the wood stove waiting for me once I finished in the outhouse.

Another perfect day even if my characters had all but shut down, sending me outside earlier than usual for a stroll up into the hills with the knife and Dad's pistol at my waist. Perhaps they needed some rest, same as my right hand. An ache had settled into the bones, and I rubbed at it absently while relaxing and allowing my body to do its thing.

A scuffle sounded outside, jolting my heart, and I stilled, not even drawing breath.

"Hello!" A deep voice called, sending a shot of adrenaline to rush through me.

Who the fuck?

I leaned forward to peer between the door cracks, quietly grasping at the pistol in its holster around my ankles with my jeans.

A man walked toward the cabin, his back toward me. Tall as fuck with broad shoulders. Dark hair, a heavy backpack strapped above a nice, round ass.

"Hello?" he called again with more of a question in his voice. "Annie?"

Roan.

"Oh, holy *hell*!" I grabbed a handful of toilet paper, cursing at my thrumming heart and shaking hand while wiping.

"Annie?" Roan called again before I could button my jeans and push open the door to escape the tight confines of the outhouse.

He peered into the cabin's window, hands framing his eyes to see the dim interior.

I swallowed a rush of saliva at the sun glinting off his dark hair, my feet frozen.

The outhouse door slammed shut behind me, jerking Roan's head my way.

I couldn't see the green of his eyes beneath his dark brow but could feel his gaze all the same. A dark beard hid his lips, but the memory of them tingled my entire body awake.

Neither of us spoke.

Neither of us moved.

Seconds slipped past, every thump of my heart a loud crash in my ears. Again, he'd made my silent, secret fantasy come to life, one I hadn't even fully admitted to myself. I'd *wanted* him to come down to the homestead. I'd hoped to see his face, hear his low voice that had always done funny things to my insides. And his lopsided smirk…yeah, I'd wanted to lay eyes on it again.

But you hate him, I reminded myself. *You refuse to forgive him.*

Pain tingled through my palm as a secondary reminder, furrowing my brow.

Best get this over with.

Lips in a thin line, I started his way, hating that he made my knees weak, that he made me want to melt like hot plastic into a puddle at his feet. Chin lifting, I marched right up to him, praying my voice wouldn't shake like my insides did.

"What are you doing here?" I asked, my tone surprisingly steady as I stopped a good ten feet away from him.

Eyes, green as spring grass peered at me, darkly lashed and full of emotion— same as they'd always been, except for the one time I had needed him most and he stared after us like a cold statue.

"Checking in on you like I'd promised your mom," he half-whispered, his voice ragged, rumbling straight to my core.

I ignored the throb he ignited between my thighs while chewing over his words. He hadn't come to see me because he couldn't stay away, because he felt the need to fall to his knees and beg forgiveness like he should have done years earlier. No. He did my mom a favor, nothing more.

Not that I want *more,* I told myself. I didn't want to like him, didn't want to *feel* want. Giving into a man meant losing my independence, and I'd sworn to myself, Mom, and my muse, that my pushover days had ended.

"Sorry to take you away from whatever work you left back home," I said, my voice biting as bitch Annie took charge, "but as you can see, I'm fine."

His gaze flickered down over me and back up, pausing on my chest.

I went without a bra, wearing nothing more than a t-shirt —which my hardening nipples poked against.

With an inner growl, I crossed my arms, covering myself from his stare.

His gaze flicked up to my eyes. "I'm sorry."

"For ogling my tits?" I shot out, never one to filter, same as Mom. Hell knew he didn't have any others to lock at—as far as I knew, anyway.

Instant jealousy sprang to life over the thought he might have gotten himself a woman somehow, someway, and no one had told me.

I hated the sudden churning feeling in my stomach more than I hated him.

Roan's throat worked, snagging my attention. His shirt opened at his neck. Tanned skin dampened with sweat called to me like a jug of ice water after a long-assed hike.

The drool factory went haywire in my mouth, and I frowned, jerking my focus back up to his face.

"I'm sorry for chasing you that day," he finally answered me, his damn eyes seemed to look straight through me like always. "For being the one responsible for your pain."

Well, shit.

I stared and considered his words long enough he shifted on his feet. Could I lower my defenses enough to believe him? Or had he really walked the distance to see about getting another taste? At least he hadn't come after me like a damn animal.

I ignored the shiver that slid through me at the thought, telling myself I couldn't allow vulnerability.

"I lost count of the skin grafts. Surgeries."

He swallowed again. "I'm so damn sorry, Annie."

"Phantom pain sometimes wakes me up from nightmares," I continued, waiting for him to fall to his knees for me.

His beard twitched like he clenched his jaw.

"It took me years before I could write legibly."

"Annie…"

"And all the typing I've been doing since arriving here is starting to ache my hand."

"I don't know what else to say."

There wasn't anything Roan Kelly could say to make it all go away, make things right, the way they used to be.

I'd learned my lesson about men, and even though Bitch Annie ruled my life, my parents had taught me proper hospitality—even if I didn't fully trust the drool-worthy man in front of me.

Letting out a huff, I eyed his dirty pants and dusty boots. He'd been walking for a couple days, three at the most. "Did you eat dinner?"

"No, ma'am."

I snorted and dropped my arms to stride toward the front door, needing some space. "Don't *ma'am* me, Roan Kelly," I shot over my shoulder. "You're the old fart around here, not me."

His lopsided smirk peeking from a face full of whiskers lit my insides, and I found myself biting back a smile of my own while turning back around and striding toward the cabin.

"Leave your boots outside!" I called to him and poured

water into the wash basin on the kitchen counter to scrub my hands. "Backpack, too!"

Vulnerability tucked itself away in my heart under lock and key, but I couldn't have him making himself too comfortable. I would feed him and send him on his way, back to his parents or back to that possible woman.

My gut churned again, and I scowled, happy I hadn't verbally accepted his apology.

"Something smells good," Roan said, ducking his head to fit through the doorway. A little taller than Dad, Roan's presence in the cabin sucked the damn oxygen right out of the small space.

My hands started shaking again, and I eyed him in my periphery while drying off. "Wash up," I half-squeaked, bringing yet another scowl to my face. "I made a stir-fry. It isn't anything spectacular, just warning you."

"Anything is better than stale sandwiches."

"Did your ma make them for you, or did you find some woman crazy enough to come to the wilderness to keep you company?" I hated the snark in my tone, but given that opportunity to find out the truth, I had to know.

I turned to find his brow furrowed as he glanced away from me. "Ma made them."

"You haven't found a woman to keep you company out here in the middle of nowhere, huh?" More snipping words, but I couldn't seem to help myself.

His green eyes raked over me again, and I fought off shivers. "No one," he choked out with regret in his gaze.

Hating that his tone made me feel like an ass, I went for the plate on the shelf. "Wash up. I'll dish the food."

He did as told while I cursed myself for being such a bitch.

But I am *a bitch. Independent and doing what* I *want. I'm no man's lackey, no man's doormat.*

I might have set the metal plates on the table a bit more firmly than necessary. I definitely clunked the serving spoon down hard on its side when emptying the rice mixture on first his plate then mine.

At least my hand didn't shake when I poured us both a glass of water.

He settled onto the chair across the table from me, and his gaze locked on my right hand grabbing for my fork.

"Do you hate me for what I did?" He asked quietly, lifting his focus to my face.

Yes.

"Accidents happen," I muttered what Dad always had said when trying to console my tears and turned my attention on my plate. The arrival of Roan had taken away my appetite, but I needed food for the hours of writing ahead.

The sooner we finished, the sooner I could shoo him out the door and kick his ass northward so I could go back to my peace and quiet.

And perhaps nurse the ache seeing him had brought back with a vengeance in my supposedly locked up heart.

6

ROAN

She hated me. Her tone, her body language, her lack of accepting my apology, said it all.

Kept my dick from jacking back up to full attention like it'd done when we'd stood in our staring match outdoors.

We ate in silence, my gaze often falling to her chest. I'd read enough old paperback romances to know what those hard points meant, but nothing that had come out of her mouth agreed with what her body suggested.

That truth kept my blood from swelling south.

"Do you hate me?" I found myself asking again, the need to know the truth like a nagging jay, insistent and annoying—but I'd promised myself I'd find a way to make things better between us.

Annie let out a sigh while poking at the rest of her food with her fork. "No. I don't hate you, Roan."

"I *am* sorry," I said yet again.

"For stealing my first kiss a day before my sweet sixteen, or for causing this?" She lifted her palm, and the sight of rippled skin, the scarring of what should have been tender flesh, knifed at my chest.

"I'll never be sorry for tasting your lips," I murmured the God's honest truth. "But that?" I nodded toward her hand as she sucked in a quick gasp over my confession. "*That*, I curse myself for every fuckin' day, Annie. Curse myself for acting like a damn animal, chasing you around that fire. A man who lost control."

"You're not sorry for kissing me."

She didn't ask a question, but I shook my head, her dark gaze ensnaring me like a hare that didn't have a damn chance at living.

"I'd do it all over again," I told her, holding that killing stare, "but take a second taste before letting you away from that tree first so I wouldn't feel the need to stalk after you for more."

Annie narrowed her eyes even though the pulse thrummed in her neck. "Well, I hope you learned your lesson about *taking* what doesn't belong to you."

Fuck.

Her sass—that mouth. My damn dick swelled, and I forced my stare on my plate, taking my time to shovel up the last couple grains of rice she'd cooked to perfection. "I learned my lesson and then some," I muttered my response. No way in hell I'd be touching a woman again without asking first. Animal or no animal sniffing out her sweetness and rising inside me to howl at the damn moon.

More than anything, I wanted to yank her over the table, scattering our dishes and the food, claim her mouth. Taste her tongue, her breath. I wanted my hands tangled in her long hair, her body under mine, her pussy wet and wanting me.

Only me.

My dick ached, the war of humanity and going all alpha animal on her gorgeous ass, created a pounding between my temples. Like a grizzly and man facing off, both acting on instinct to survive for another chance to mate.

Annie was a strong woman regardless of her small size, and considering our past, I knew she wouldn't want my inner beast let loose. He wouldn't ask before taking, and I'd promised myself to never allow him to take charge.

The war settled in my head, my dick relented by the time I finished eating. I carried my empty plate and fork to the wash bucket, taking my time cleaning up my things like Ma had taught me to do. "Thank you for dinner."

"Yep." She stepped up beside me, her plate outstretched.

I took it from her without looking her in the face, quietly washing up her things as well. Did she know I would move mountains for her? Divert the river's flow with my bare fuckin' hands if given the chance? Fight against my animal instincts whenever she drew near—because it's what she preferred?

"Coffee?" she asked quietly, sending a shot of happiness through me.

She's not tossing me out on my ass. "Please."

A half-hour of silence later, we sat out on the stoop, mugs in hand, both of us staring off into the distance.

Awareness of her closeness, the sweet, natural scent of her reaching my nose, made sitting still difficult. Made keeping the need to claim and fuck a battle once more raging in my damn head. I clutched at my mug, my teeth grit when not sipping the black brew she'd made strong, just how I liked it.

Movement in my periphery jerked my head to my right—fuckin' spider scuttled close to my foot, whipping all thoughts from my head like a blizzard's wind. I kept still rather than holler and jump up, turned my stare right on him, my heart thumping…waiting.

Close enough.

I held my mug off to the side and let loose with my boot, stomping that fucker clear into the ground, twisting my foot back and forth, making sure to grind him into the dust, a little coffee sloshing out of my mug.

Annie giggled.

"What?" I lifted my foot to make sure he was gone. Fuckin' carcass clung to my heel. "Fuckin' thing!" I shook my foot, and Annie giggled again. "Fuck." I rubbed my sole back and forth on the ground until the damn thing lay curled in on itself beside a pebble.

"Still have a phobia over spiders, huh?"

I grunted an affirmative and sipped my coffee, glad to see my damn hand didn't shake.

She huffed another bit of laughter, but I could find humor in the moment. Hated fuckin' spiders with a damn passion.

"We had good times out here, didn't we?" Annie's quiet whisper barely registered a few moments later as I swallowed my coffee.

"We did."

"The best was when your family came down here to visit, and the three of us camped beneath the stars."

She, Junior, and I had been close back then. And more than once, I'd woken up to find her snuggled closer to me than her brother on her opposite side. Between us to keep her safe, Junior had said that first time, and I never argued. Even back then, I'd have done anything to be closer to her.

That first summer my family had made the trek for a week-long visit with the Charrans, she'd been thirteen to my sixteen. And for the following two years, for six nights, I got the privilege of sleeping beside her. Staring at her profile lit by the moon while her brother snored from her other side.

The fourth year, her family flew in and camped out on our

homestead. It'd been their last night with us, and I'd been at my rope's end, having endured her teasing glances, her flirting, and sassing off at me for years.

An untried man of nineteen, never having tasted a woman before—she'd pushed me to the edge, and that sassy smirk she'd tossed my way…

———

"She's asking for it," Junior grumbled at me as we sat by the fire and his sister sauntered toward the trees behind our house even though darkness had crept across the sky.

"Asking for what?" I asked, my gaze glued to her backside.

"Dude, you're a moron."

I backhanded his arm, and he laughed. "It's close enough to midnight. Go give her that sweet sixteen kiss she's all but begging you for."

I hesitated. "You're telling me to go kiss your sister."

"I'd rather it be someone I trust than some asshole from school."

Junior trusted me. My chest fuckin' ached.

"Go on." Junior encouraged with a smirk similar to his sisters. "Don't want her trampling off through the trees out here in the dark, anyway. Dad would have my hide if he knew."

I hopped up, my dick ready to lead the way.

"Roan."

A quick glance down at Junior paused my suddenly itching feet.

He guzzled down the rest of his water before tossing the plastic bottle into the fire. "Hurt her—and I'll kill you."

He trusted me but loved her more. Blood and all, I

wouldn't expect any less. Lips in a tight line, I dipped my head in agreement. "Won't," I managed to rasp out, my need quickly taking me after her.

"Where'd you go, Roan?" Annie's soft voice pulled me back to the present.

I shifted to relieve the renewed ache in my groin. "Back to that night. Going after you when I shouldn't have. Taking rather than asking, then becoming nothing more than a damn animal."

"It was everything a girl's first kiss should be, though."

I angled away to get a better look at her face. Her beautiful profile. Long lashes and pert nose. Full lips slightly parted.

"It was good?" I asked, my mouth quirking up at the ego boost.

"For a first kiss," she said, smirking sideways at me. "Wouldn't call it earth shattering or anything." The lifted mug hid her mouth I couldn't keep from staring at even after she swallowed. "Roan?" Those lips…

"Yeah?" I rasped, shifting yet again while continuing to stare.

"Drink your coffee."

"Yes, ma'am."

She elbowed me, sloshing my coffee onto my thigh. "Shit!" She giggled as I hopped up even though the coffee wasn't hot enough to burn. "You, um… Need to go take care of that?"

Annie stared at my groin rather than the coffee spot on my pants—a mere four or so feet away from her face.

Fuck.

I attempted to work some moisture to my mouth, my dick jerking beneath her gaze. "Yeah," I rasped out, needing to take care of both the wetness and the leaking length strangling to death inside my pants.

"Go on, then." She sipped her coffee as though unaffected, her focus flitting beyond me. "Our outhouse is your outhouse."

Grimacing, I set down my mug and made for the privacy of the small bathroom, still hard and aching when I should have been embarrassed at her unfiltered, flippant remarks over my hard dick.

At least I didn't groan out her name loud enough for her to hear while emptying my balls.

7

———

ANNIE

His presence had worn on me, reminding me too much of good times, laughter, and innocent happiness. That lopsided smirk, those piercing eyes, had softened me to the point I lost the bitchy tone and *wanted* to reminisce.

I acted unaffected by his closeness, though. Feigned indifference to mine and his obvious discomfort beside me on the stoop. He'd shifted enough I knew how I affected his body, same as he did mine. And when he stood? Holy hell, the length on that man did more than funny things to my belly.

My pussy spasmed as I laid in bed, staring at the loft logs overhead the bed I'd made my own. Heat flushed through me, and I grumbled, tossing the blanket off my overly warm body.

His fault.

Goddamnit, my face hurt from scowling.

He slept outside beneath the stars, beside the fire pit. Seeing as how we'd stayed up until long after midnight talking about the good old days, I couldn't very well tell him to scamper off on his way home.

But I hadn't been about to invite him to crash in the loft.

It was bad enough having him in close proximity, smelling all mouth-watering like the outdoors and musky man.

My damn pussy spasmed again, flatlining my lips. A war battled inside my head, part of me loving the company, longing for more hours with him, the other, mainly my muse, bitched that she hadn't gotten any words in that night. Roan had been a distraction. A gorgeous, rugged, delicious-looking distraction my fingers itched to touch, my tongue—

"Oh, shut the hell up, already," I grumbled to myself, flopping onto my belly. "I'll feed him breakfast then send him on his way."

Feeling a bit better by having a plan, I finally found sleep.

———

"So why are you out here all alone?"

I shoved a spoonful of raisin oatmeal into my mouth so I wouldn't have to answer Roan right away.

He swigged his coffee and waited, those damn eyes of his staring, probing enough I shifted on my wooden seat. So much for feigning indifference.

"I need to get some writing done."

He took another sip while I dished up another bite. He'd finished a few seconds earlier, leaning back in his chair all comfy-like, as though he intended to settle in for a nice long stay.

Not happening.

"You seem sad."

"Nope." I ate another bite, not able to give him my attention if I had intentions of getting sustenance in my body for the long writing hours ahead of me.

"Annie."

Fine. I glanced up, an eyebrow raised in question while chewing.

"You're an open book." He leaned onto the table, crossing his arms, coffee pushed to the side while peering at my face. "And you're full of shit."

Nosey bastard never did hold back punches of honesty.

I figured I might as well sate his curiosity that had always been bad enough to kill a cat so I could get him to leave.

"My boyfriend broke up with me, broke my heart, I need time to myself—*alone*—and so here I am. Happy now?" I snipped the words.

A frown flitted over his brow and smoothed out, his face going all blank as a freshly cleaned blackboard on my ass. For as emotional as Roan was sometimes, I didn't think him capable of hiding his thoughts from his face. "You had a boyfriend?"

His reserved tone gave him away, though—jealousy, that gut churning feeling I'd felt the day before thinking about another woman having his mouth.

I hated that my insides purred and turned my thoughts on the fact he chose to focus on that rather than how I'd empha-sized *alone* in my statement.

"Yes. For four years, all through college," I answered, watching his face closely.

"Did you let him fuck you?" He asked, all nonchalant like he didn't care either way—but the tightness in his voice gave him away again.

"What the hell, Roan?" I hopped up and stalked to the wash basin with my bowl and spoon even though I hadn't finished my breakfast. "You've got no right to ask me such a thing. And being a wild mountain man who doesn't know the etiquette of society is no excuse, either, so don't blow bullshit my way."

"Did you?"

I tossed my spoon into the bucket, splattering water across the counter, and turned, hands on my hips. My glare didn't back him down, didn't so much as twitch his face. "Yes, I let him fuck me. Countless times."

"Was it any good?"

"The fuck!"

"Were his kisses earth shattering?"

"Goddamn you, Roan," I growled, snatched up his empty bowl, and spun back to the bucket. "I'm not going to discuss this and stroke your ego."

Shit. An admission without freaking meaning to—and *stroke* all in one. My insides warmed through at the memory of that ridge I'd seen the night before, and how my fingers had itched to touch, my tongue to taste.

Roan went silent, thank fuck, and I washed our dishes, giving me time to calm my hormones down.

He grabbed the dishtowel and dried what I washed, his warmth mere inches from me jacking my heart rate back up. "So, you're still writing."

"Yeah," I didn't hesitate to answer since he so kindly changed the topic.

"What for?"

My chin lifted automatically as I glanced over at him. Would he disappoint like everyone but my family? "I'm going to become a published author. Hit every bestseller list there is."

His nose crinkled and brow furrowed like he thought I was out of my mind, but I shouldn't have been surprised. I'd gotten the same response from my ex.

A pain rippled through my chest as I waited for Roan to next laugh at my silliness—same as my ex—and I turned back to the wash bucket to hide the pain I couldn't keep from my face.

"You always told great stories. I've missed them."

Tears stung my eyes and thickened my throat—then I reminded myself of his jealousy seconds earlier, and what he must truly be after to spew lies like that.

I didn't respond, simply put some space between us, grabbing my sweatshirt to trek to the outhouse once finished. I opened my mouth to thank him for his visit, but that I had work to do.

He beat me to voicing a word. "You must be tired of canned meat," he murmured, all kind and sweet, like he genuinely cared. "Want to go set a couple snares? See what we can find for dinner?"

I snapped my lips shut and eyed him. Yet another stare down escalated where neither of us yielded. A carnivore through and through, the idea of fresh meat tempted me to give into his manipulation in getting me to allow him to stay longer. I'd been at the keyboard for how many days straight? One full day of rest wouldn't hurt considering all those yet ahead of me.

"Fine. We'll set snares, and you can stay for dinner tomorrow night, too."

His smirk and the glint in his eyes sent my stomach through a roller coaster loop, and I spun away before I smiled back at him.

8

—————

ROAN

Tackling Annie's stubbornness was no easy feat, but I managed to weasel another day of being with her. I thought I'd managed to become her friend the night before, sitting out by a fire and talking about the good old days, laughing again over damn spider stories, but with the sunrise and my prodding into her life, came the walls again.

As for my prying, I couldn't help myself. The idea of another man getting after her—fuckin' *having* her with her consent—twisted my guts up in a tight knot. I'd held in my growl and the need to take, claim her as my own, at her admission, but barely. Already skittish around me, Annie would send me packing if I let my instincts rule.

Best to stick to being her friend and not hoping for more.

"Do you still love it out here like you did when you were a kid?" I asked, hating the silence between us as we hiked away from the river.

She walked ahead of me, and I studied her profile as she gazed from left to right and back again, ever watchful as a woman of the wilderness ought to be. "It's quiet and peaceful, but I miss the noise sometimes."

49

If she missed noise, she'd never want to live in the middle of nowhere full time. "What else do you miss?" I had to ask in order to keep my hopes clamped down shut that Annie could ever be what I wanted, what I needed in a woman.

"Running water."

"That was kinda nice," I agreed, remembering the shower I'd enjoyed while in town. "But at least you don't need to worry about contaminates and filtering if you're pulling water straight from the river flowing off pristine mountains."

"I miss not needing sunlight to fill the battery packs," she continued as though I hadn't pointed out a positive of living off grid. "Electricity. Hot water on demand."

She'd had them too long to give them up for a mere chickadee like myself. I scuffed at a rock on the trail we followed.

"Fresh eggs. Chicken and beef. Refrigerator to keep wine cold." She sighed. "A freezer."

"The cave in the hillside does a good job," I tossed out, desperate to find something beyond the cons.

"It's not the same."

We hiked the rest of the way in silence since I didn't need to hear any more negativity over the fact that what I enjoyed, what I had, would never be enough for her. As though I needed the reminder.

We took turns setting snares, and I stood back and admired her work, efficient hands, the wires set with no questioning glances my way to make sure she'd done it right. She'd had a good teacher in Brock.

Annie also carried her phone, a knife, and pistol on her hip, same as she'd had on her the day before just for a quick walk to the outhouse.

Smart woman, my Annie.

Not mine.

Jaw clenched, I butchered the two grouse I'd shot for our dinner since the snares would need a day or two. Nothing like weaseling my way in for a longer visit. But how much agony could I take? She might not hate me, but she wanted me gone.

No question about it.

Staying would only make my longing for her worse like Ma suggested, but I couldn't keep from finding reasons to push her into letting me stay.

The entire next day I chopped up firewood while she sat inside and worked on her novel. She'd said she wanted to be a published author one day, which I didn't doubt she had the talent to do, but how did one go about it? My brow furrowed again same as when she'd told me the foreign idea. Couldn't make sense of it in my brain and I'd been too embarrassed by my ignorance to ask.

Did you just take your manuscript to a publisher? Did you have to somehow create the paperback and then submit it? Take a stack of papers to a publishing company and watch them bind it together into a book?

I had no fuckin' clue, just knew I loved to read whatever Jessie brought to us from the library.

If anyone could fulfill that dream, I knew Annie could. She'd always told the best stories, just like I'd told her the night before while we washed up our dinner dishes. I hoped she did. I hoped she sold thousands of copies and became known world-wide, hitting all those seller lists she dreamed about.

She deserved it.

Sweat dripped off me as I swung the axe over and over, rebuilding the stockpile Brock had readied the summer before that Annie had dug into.

I'd told her it was my favor in return for the home cooked meals, so she wouldn't have to replace what she would use over the summer even though I knew Brock wouldn't expect it from her.

My mouth dried out after about an hour, and I went inside for some water.

Annie rummaged in a bin beside the bed, not giving me the time of day, so I enjoyed the sight of her backside while chugging down my drink.

"Enjoying the view?" she asked without turning.

I jerked my focus off her and turned to refill my glass. No point in lying, I went with honesty. "Always."

She made some sort of humphing noise under her breath, and stalked past me, heading to the door I'd left open. She held a towel and change of clothes. "I'm going to the river to bathe, but don't get any ideas. Your *view* has officially ended."

I bit back a grin and kept my thoughts to myself. I'd peeked as a teenager once when she'd been fifteen or so, and I would fuckin' peek again given the chance. Being sneaky and quiet when hunting prey came easy to the animal inside me, so I agreed to let him out —but just for a bit of fun.

Annie headed down the pebbled path to the river, then southward to hide herself behind some shrubs. The distance was far enough she might not hear the lack of an axe thunking into wood, but with the lack of rain, the low river, there wouldn't be as much muffling noise from the water swirling around her to help my cause.

Fuck it.

I split three logs, left the axe embedded in another, and started my way through the brush to sate my curiosity.

A good fifty yards or so from the riverbank, I caught sight of her through the brush. Fuckin' naked as the day she'd been born. Pale skin, dark hair appearing black by being soaked with river water and hanging clear to her flared hips.

Water lapped at the apex of her thighs as she lathered up her hands with a bar of soap. Eyes closed, her brow smoothed of the scowl that seemed permanent since my arrival, she ran her hand and the soap over her arms. Her taut belly. The swell of her breasts.

Fuck, had she filled out in all the right places since I'd last seen her naked.

I pressed hard against my dick with my palm, trying to talk myself down, but who was I kidding? I'd come down to the riverside to watch Annie bathe to give me a vision to remember whenever my dick ached with need and to give me a gorgeous sight to jerk off to.

She took her time smoothing her hands over her breasts, thumbs rubbing her nipples until her lips parted.

I stared while yanking open my pants to spring myself free.

Curses muttered through my head at the amount of pre-cum ready and waiting for me. The wet schlick of my fist fucking my dick filled my ears as Annie continued on with her bathing, coming closer to shore to wash her legs— between those fuckin' pale thighs and patch of dark hair.

She tossed the soap ashore and waded back into deeper water. A quick submerge, and she came back up, smoothing back her hair—but she stayed put as though the freezing cold water didn't bother her.

I jacked my length slowly, dragging out every upward swipe, gathering more pre-cum that leaked in abundance.

Every downward stroke tightened my balls higher against my groin, and I clenched my jaw to keep from blowing. Making a damn fantasy come to life and linger as long as possible.

She came closer to shore and sat on the boulder where her clothing waited.

I hastened my movement, wanting to finish before she covered up, but rather than dress, she lounged back on the rock and closed her eyes.

My hand slowed once more, realizing the sun must have warmed the boulder beneath her. She didn't dry off, but laid there in profile, her nipples still pointed.

Fuck.

Two slow, wet strokes, and I paused, desperate to keep from coming.

Annie smoothed a hand up over her belly as though wiping water beads away, but continued up over her breast closest to me, thumbing at her nipple again.

Every muscle inside my body tensed, and I squeezed the head of my dick to keep from shooting my spunk into the brush. Staring. Breath held…

Her other hand eased between her thighs, and they spread wide—but fuckin' hid from my view. A slow stroke of her palm over the bit of hair there, and she lifted her hips as though desperate for her own touch.

I gulped as she reached down farther.

Annie's lips parted, her hand moving in time with the steady upward rise of her hips.

She fucked her fingers.

"Fuck," I gasped, "…oh *fuck*."

The sounds of the river kept me from hearing whatever whimpers or moans escaped her plump lips, but I could imagine them—and my hand began to move in time with hers.

Fucking my hand. Imagining her pussy squeezed me. Milked my length.

I bit the inside of my cheek to keep from shouting as my balls let loose, spurt after spurt jerking my hips toward her.

My ears buzzed, my heart thumped damn near hard enough to burst from my chest.

A deep groan escaped through my nose as the last bit of cum dribbled down to coat my hand.

Still, I stared, watched as she writhed. Bit her lower lip. Back bowed off the rock— Annie shuddered, her hips held up and shaking, her feet arching her lower half higher as though seeking more than what her fingers could offer.

I wanted to offer the use of my dick that stayed hard in my hand. Fuck, did I want to offer the use of my body to give her what she chased.

But it wouldn't be enough.

"Fucking hell." I ripped my stare off Annie and bent to wipe my hands on the dry lichen. Grimacing, I tucked my dick away, set on returning to the job I'd started a few hours earlier.

Balls sated.

Mind filled with lust.

Heart aching over knowing *I* would never be enough even if my dick would fill her pussy if given the chance.

9

—————

ANNIE

I could feel Roan's gaze as obvious as the sun beating down on the rock beneath me. But I'd felt it long before I decided to be cruel and tease him, tempt the animal I knew lay inside him.

The water had lazed between my thighs, the height just enough to kiss at my lower lips. Between the cool laps and warm air, my arousal spiked.

I'd been writing another scene that had fallen short, so I gave into what I'd done my first day on the homestead and lived out the fantasy in my head before rewriting. The scene ended up perfect and left me hot and bothered.

Needing to bathe anyway, I used that as my excuse to escape the immediate vicinity, and good thing I had, because Roan came in for a drink without knocking, exactly when I would have been sprawled on the bed with the rubber dildo shoved up my sopping pussy.

Down to the river I went, and I wondered if he would follow like he'd done that one time when I'd been fifteen.

I'd seen him in the brush that summer, but the naughtiness of what he did, his sneaking around as an eighteen-

56

year-old to watch a minor wash herself... It had turned me on.

I never told a soul.

While covert glances toward shore didn't reveal Roan watching me after that scene heating me up, I pretended he did. I enjoyed the cool water's kisses entirely too much. Washed my body imagining it was his hands on me—and my arousal took over my body enough the cold water didn't bother me for once.

But the need to be cruel in retaliation for what he'd done to me, or so I told myself, laid me out on in profile to him on the rock, situated so it would be a tease rather than an eyeful of what he couldn't have.

My messing with fire of a different sort certainly wasn't smart, but I couldn't help myself. Arousal slickened me beyond what I'd experienced before, easing the way for two fingers deep inside my core. I pinched my nipple, rode my fingers, grinding my palm against my clit.

A deep groan sounded—faint, but to my right—and I *knew* he watched. My heart sped, and a rush of wetness dripped from my body. Lower lip between my teeth, I came hard and fast, my fingers falling short of what I'd hoped for.

Climax, but not enough. I needed more than mere fingers.

Gasping for breath, I lay lax on the rock, wishing I'd brought the dildo along with me. Half-wishing Roan had come crashing through the brush he'd hid in and taken what didn't belong to him.

Another swell of arousal swept up from my toes at the thought. My mindset refused to submit to a man weaseling his way into my life, my pants, my pussy, but hell if the idea of him giving over to that feral part of him that had chased me eight years earlier...

A shudder rippled over me, and I moved off the rock,

needing to wash between my thighs again, wash my mind of such fantasies I told myself I didn't really want.

———

I didn't tease him when I returned to the cabin to find him still splitting wood. Sitting back down at my computer, I forced myself to write—and fell flat with the words.

Roan needed to leave. He distracted my body and my muse to the point I grew annoyed.

He went to check on our snares in late afternoon, returning with two hares which he roasted outside over an open fire.

I fried up some potatoes, heated canned green beans, and we sat in tense silence on opposite sides of the fire, eating what we'd cooked together. Neither of us mentioned what had happened by the river, but I caught him looking at my hands rather than my lips like usual whenever we ate.

I'd been nothing but a tease throughout our younger years, tempting a full-grown man when I hadn't a clue about reality. I'd all but asked for him to take—not that it excused his behavior.

Still.

The naughty man made it too easy to keep on with what I'd always done, and to distract him like he'd been doing to me.

Grease smeared over my fingers, so I watched him through my lashes while sucking them clean.

He stilled, potato-speared fork inches from his mouth.

I popped my fingers from my mouth and flicked my tongue between them, letting out a slight moan—*because I'm a bitch.*

My pussy pulsed as his Adam's apple bobbed, but his humanity stayed in control. A covert glance let me know he must be uncomfortable with the thick bulge trapped against his thigh.

No way he wore tighty whities with where that python had stretched. Boxers? Commando?

Arousal coated my panties, and I hurried to finish my food.

He insisted on washing the dishes. I dried.

And still silence reigned.

"Be back in a bit," he stated gruffly when we finished, before stalking out the door without looking at me.

I watched through the front window as he made for the trees rather than the outhouse like I'd expected.

My curiosity got the best of me, and I slipped outside, headed toward the outhouse like I had to pee—until he disappeared into the brush. I angled his way and hurried after him, my heart in my throat, arousal strumming me tight. Fighting to keep my breaths quiet, I snuck along the path he'd taken, every step set down with care. Silent.

Roan leaned his forearm against a tree down by the river —close to where he must have hidden in the brush—his back toward me, but his other arm flexed, worked, like he jerked himself off.

I held still and watched, same as he'd done with me earlier, my pussy weeping for whatever he packed in front of his round, thrusting ass. He hadn't even dropped his pants, just jerked off through the gaping front.

As though desperate.

I fisted my hands at my sides to keep from running them over myself where I throbbed with wet need.

"Fuck." He grunted, the sound easing more slickness from my core. Another curse, and he tipped his head back, the wet sounds of his fucking his fist like the most sinful delight a woman could imagine.

My mouth flooded with drool.

Adrenaline damn near flooded my blood stream.

"Annie…" he groaned out my name, and a spurt of white shot past the tree's trunk. Three more grunts, and he let out an unsteady breath, his forehead falling against his forearm resting on the tree, his hips stilling.

I turned and crept back the way I'd come, silent as a mouse, and scurrying just as fast.

I'd read my fair share of erotic stories. Watched porn in the excuse of needing inspiration. Nothing prepared me for the reality of Roan's sexuality. The sounds coming from his lips, my name on his lips as he came…

A shudder rippled over me when I slipped back into the cabin, my pulse thrumming.

Roan needed to go before temptation to sprawl on my back and *offer* myself proved too much to deny myself what he wanted, and what I knew would send me spiraling right back to the Annie I used to be. Compliant, putting her dreams on hold.

No more.

Bitch Annie needed to stay strong.

10

ROAN

I slept like shit on the dry ground, beneath a star-lit sky. We needed rain, and I needed to leave.

Annie hadn't spoken two words to me once I got back from relieving the ache in my balls. She sat with that damn computer on her lap, and I left her alone, getting the hint. She didn't want company.

Whittling out by the fire filled the time until I didn't feel like a fool curling up too early in the bed I'd made for myself outside. I managed some shut eye but woke the next morning with a raging hard on.

Annie didn't look like she'd slept much better, her eyes tired, her shoulders stooped.

"How's the writing going?" I asked as she handed me a cup of coffee. I'd shot off against the same tree as the day before a few minutes earlier, needing to get rid of my stiff dick before approaching the cabin.

She let out a heavy sigh between parted lips. "It's not."

"How come?"

A shrug lifted and dropped her shoulders as she turned her back on me. "Oatmeal?"

"That'd be great." I studied her backside for a few seconds but forced my mind off having it. "Maybe you need to take a nice long hike. Clear your head. Find inspiration."

"Oh, I have inspiration, alright," she muttered, but didn't clang anything around like she usually did when she used that tone.

"I'm more than happy to help you work it out if talking it over would help."

"Work it out," she repeated—and snorted.

I raised an eyebrow, gaze plastering to her pert little ass again as she bent to pick up the bucket of water I'd brought up from the river. "Need any help?"

Another snort, and I scratched the back of my neck, wondering what the hell she had going on in her head.

"Oh. Hello, there." She bent again and picked up something too small for me to see. Standing, she shot me a smirk over her shoulder.

"What?"

"Got myself a little friend. Want to see him?"

I glanced at her hand—a spider crawled over her palm. "Get that fuckin' thing away from me."

"Ooo!" She made like a ghost, waving her spider-hand at me.

I hopped back, shoving the chair I'd been sitting on between us. "Annie," I warned, my tone low.

"What?" Her dark eyes twinkled as she pretended to study the spider, holding her hand close to her face. "I don't think he likes you, Mr. Scary Spider. Maybe you ought to go make friends."

"Mr. Scary *Spider* is fine right where he is," I grumbled, hating such a tiny thing made me a chicken shit.

She fuckin' tossed him at me, and I hollered, thrashing my arm, and ducking away. Her laughter burst through my chest like a beam of light, but I narrowed my gaze and jumped after her once making sure the too-many-legged creature scuttled up the log wall behind me.

A shriek of laughter, and she bolted toward the door, getting outside, and slamming it back at me before I could cross the threshold.

"You're going to pay for that!" I hollered, giving her a few feet head start—and I took off in a burst of adrenaline, chasing—because no coals remained in the fire pit, and because I'd fuckin' had enough.

My control snapped.

Annie laughed and sped toward the brush, her long dark hair flying wild behind her, arms pumping, feet kicking up pebbles and dust. With a growl, I closed the distance between us, my boots pounding into the dry ground.

She had to know I would chase her.

She had to know she wouldn't outrun me.

She had to know her actions would bring consequences.

Sassy little Annie Charran had known exactly what she'd done.

Time to show her what happens when a man reaches the end of his rope.

I swept her off her feet with a single arm around her waist. She shrieked with laughter, and I growled again, spinning her, and pinning her against the tree I'd soaked with my cum not even an hour earlier.

I hope the wetness soaks clear through her clothes, coats her skin—

Every soft inch of her pressed against my hard front, and her smile slowly faded as we both gasped for breath. Faces inches apart. Lips close—so damn close I could taste her sweet breath on my tongue.

My hips moved on their own, grinding my aching length

against her belly. I wanted to rut into her like a wild animal. Bite her pale skin, bruise it beneath my hand grasping at her ass. My other hand tangled in her hair, tilting her head back even farther.

I stared at her parted lips, memories of their softness, their taste slamming into my brain.

"Don't," Annie whispered.

One kiss, one more taste… I leaned in.

"Roan. Please."

I clamped my eyelids shut, clenched my jaw, and tipped my forehead against hers. Breathed her in for a few seconds longer—and stepped back because it's what she'd asked. What she wanted. And thank fuck her stating my name gave me enough control to give it to her.

"I-I need to go." Swallowing, I forced myself back another step, giving her the space she required even though her teasing, her throbbing pulse, and straining nipples suggested otherwise. "Check the snares. Head out." I scrambled for words while an emotional knife stabbed at my chest.

"I think that would be for the best," Annie whispered, her dark eyes glancing away rather than allowing me to read why she denied me. Us.

Fuck.

I spun around, hands fisted, teeth clenched. Took me all of two minutes to grab my pack, my shit, and head west, straight up into the hills—Annie hadn't even returned.

Checking snares. I snorted. I needed to disappear for more than a few hours. I needed my wilderness, my home. Praying like hell it would be enough, I didn't look back, not knowing when I could *go* back and be able to keep from taking what I'd become desperate for.

11

ANNIE

I lay curled up on the bed, staring at the blackened fireplace. Roan had left like I'd told myself I wanted him to. He'd left me alone, disappearing up into the hills.

And I'd watched him go until he passed from sight.

He didn't turn to wave, didn't say goodbye.

For the best.

So why did my damn heart hurt? Why did my eyes sting like I wanted to cry?

Fucking hormones, that's what. I rolled to my back and pressed the heels of my hands against my eyes, breathing slowly, determined to not shed tears because of P-fucking-MS. I wanted him. I didn't want him.

The fuck was wrong with me? Teasing him like I'd been doing, and then telling him no?

Bitch, indeed.

I'm afraid to trust him.

I blew out a heavy exhale and flopped my arms onto the mattress beside me. Yes, I liked Roan Kelly. Loved him as a child when I'd first seen him, and since he'd shown up at the homestead a couple days earlier, he'd been nothing but kind and in control. More than a bit nosey, but when hadn't he been? Always asking questions, wanting to know about town, what it felt like to have friends, asking Junior about cars and high school.

Dad had flown him in that one time to find out for himself, but he hadn't stayed long and had never returned. I recalled watching him stride up through the hills, every bit of clothing on him blending into the ground, the shrubs, the trees. Like he belonged, like he was Mother's Nature's child —or lover. One she held close to her chest, either way.

"He loves it out here. He belongs here."

It must be nice to know where one belonged. I thought I'd build a home, a possible family with my ex Justin, but he'd opened my eyes to the fact it would be at my expense. At least he'd broken my heart before we got married. I would have been tied then. I took vows seriously, took relationships seriously, which was why I'd never slept with anyone before him, and no one since.

So where do I belong?

I studied the logs overhead as sleep evaded me—yet again.

"In front of a computer," I muttered to myself. "Writing instead of daydreaming, fantasizing, or watching Roan out the damn window. *That's* where I belong right now."

Talk about a distraction. Even the memories of our few days together lay heavy on my mind, squashing whatever attempts my muse might make to engage my creativity.

Heat prickled my skin, and I climbed out of bed to open the windows, hoping for a cross breeze. We could have done with a bit of rain. A lot, actually. I'd never seen the river so low, the ground around the homestead so dry.

I flopped back on the bed and stared some more, trying to force my thoughts to stay focused on the next scene I needed to write. I fell asleep before inspiration struck, but when I woke in the morning, my muse whispered I needed to get my ass in gear.

Sipping my coffee, I stared at the open document on my screen, still unsure.

Just start already.

Lips pressed tight, I put my fingers on the keys—and started spewing shit until my stubborn daydreaming gave way to my antsy muse.

Four hours later, my stomach grumbled, and I took a quick break to eat something. I went straight back to it, the damn having opened, one I'd created myself by allowing my mind to veer off the goal path I'd set before me in coming to the homestead.

This time is about me. What I want. To meet my goal and accomplish my dream.

Nothing and no one was going to stop me.

12

ROAN

For two days straight, I frowned. Muttered curses. Fucked my hand and drained my dick dry until chafed and sore. The peace and quiet around me didn't soothe my mind like it usually did. The critters and birds didn't lighten my mental load when they broke the silence. No sunrise or sunset filled me with the sense of rightness I always felt while out and away from the homestead.

I ached for Annie. Her smirk. Her laughter. Even her damn sassy tone and attitude.

And her teasing? Recalling her tongue flicking around her fingers like I wanted to do between her thighs stiffened me every time, leaving me unfulfilled.

I got my fill of roasted meat, though. Then dreamed about her lips, her breasts with their tight buds, the hidden part of her beneath that trimmed patch of hair at the top of her thighs.

Woke both mornings hard and cursing.

The third morning, I ached, but more than just for Annie. My muscles, my joints, hurt like I'd spent a full day felling trees and carrying lengths back to the homestead, and my head fuckin' throbbed like someone had smashed a hammer against my temple. Rather than bake the heat of the sun already shining down on me, I shivered inside my clothes. Cold. Teeth chattering.

Fuckin' fever.

I closed my eyes, trying to work some saliva into my mouth. Never been so damn thirsty.

I grabbed my canteen I'd filled at a stream the day before and guzzled it down, the coldness rushing straight to my empty stomach.

Teeth clenched to keep from chattering, I forced myself to get up. Lace my boots.

I hadn't seen any evidence of an infected hare I'd skinned or eaten, but I didn't bother stripping down to check for a tick bite, either. I'd been hit with tularemia some way or another —and I needed to get back to Annie quick as fuck.

Surely her Ma and Pa had the antibiotics most backwoods people knew to keep on hand in the rare occurrence they encountered an infected animal or diseased tick made a snack of their blood.

My hands shook as I struggled to pack my bag. Strapping it onto my back and standing to my full height drained me of whatever energy I'd stored while sleeping.

I'd felt fine the night before, but I knew if I didn't get antibiotics soon, I might not make it another night or two. I headed toward the Charran homestead, mindlessly putting one foot in front of the other for what seemed hours, the sun hot on my head, my muscles twitching in an attempt to heat up my already burning body.

So cold.

Teeth chattering…feet stumbling.

She smiled at me from across the fire, her smirk a tempta-tion to crawl over Junior and kiss those lips.

My head spun and my shoulder crashed against a tree.

Soft lips opening beneath mine, our tongues tasting...

I sprawled down face first to the ground. Time ticked slow, slower than my racing heart.

Thirsty.

Warm water trickled between my dry lips.

My canteen emptied, but I couldn't head off course for more. Tossing it aside, I blinked in the sunlight, unable to keep my head from spinning. My teeth clanking together rattled my pounding brain, and I wrapped my arms around myself.

One step. Another.

Need Annie. Need her holding me. Need her hands grasping at my hair, her whimpers in my mouth again...

Darkness came over me for a time.

Sleep?

Annie's hair tangled in my fingers, and I studied my dirtied hands in bright sunlight—but no soft, dark strands weaved between their slowly wiggling lengths.

Blinking at the sky, I stumbled in a circle, chasing the sun and its warmth.

Find Annie.

Ignoring the sun that did nothing to warm my insides, I turned eastward, knowing what I needed lay that way.

More darkness—perhaps I slept after all.

My head lay in a fog, rarely rising to reality even though I fought to think straight. See clearly.

I stumbled around a hill, and the Charran homestead came into view. The cabin wavered in my sight as I tried to work saliva to life in my mouth. A few fumbled footsteps, and I fell again, straight to my knees.

Pain radiated upward, and I leaned forward onto my hands to rest.

For a moment.

The dark sky spread overhead when I squinted up through heavy eyelids what seemed days later. Dried as the ground beneath me, my lips cracked, my tongue like sandpaper when I attempted to lick moisture over them.

Pushing onto my haunches, I swayed and shivered, trying to focus eyes and a mind fuzzy with fever.

One step at a time. Just one.

I slipped my bag from my back and crawled.

One yard.

Two.

"Annie," I croaked, my voice barely a whisper.

She arched on the rock, the hand between her thighs moving in time with my thrusting hips as I fucked my hand.

Annie.

A light shone in the window, a sweet ray of hope in the dimness of the Alaskan night, bringing a bit of clarity to my reality. My hands bled, every rock and twig digging into my knees worsening the pain from having fallen dozens of times.

Hot. Fuckin' hot.

I ripped off my sweatshirt.

My head pounded—drove me fucking mad.

My shirt fell to the dust, too.

I crawled a dozen feet, my mind wavering back to the sight of Annie in the river. Her breasts, her white thighs, the long tresses cascading down her back.

Shivers wracked me, cracking my teeth together. Never ending.

The dick between my weak thighs ached to have her regardless of my pain.

Closer still—yet so fuckin' far.

"Annie," I croaked again, but unless she had a window open, she wouldn't hear. *Rifle…shoot the rifle.*

My bloodied hands roamed over my chest, my shoulder, numbly searching bare skin.

Gone.

Head hanging, I dragged myself forward what seemed like miles until I collapsed onto my side. Hard metal dug into my hip. I rolled to my back with a groan, fumbled at my waist —and found my pistol strapped tight in its holster. Hands shaking, I unsnapped the hook. Chambered with shaking hands. Shot into the air, my grip weak and wavering.

I turned my head and fought to focus on the cabin's front door...so much closer than I'd thought. How had I crawled so far?

An angel appeared in the window, and I smiled so damn hard, my face hurt. "Annie."

I waved the gun, my hand shaking like mad.

Shot again.

The door wrenched open.

"What the fuck!" Annie hollered, sprinting toward me. Barefoot. Long t-shirt. Dark hair streaming behind her.

Annie. My beautiful, sweet Annie.

Still smiling, I closed my eyes and rested, knowing she was strong enough to save me.

13

ANNIE

Holy *fucking* hell, Roan burned up.

"Talk to me, Roan." I patted his face, turned him toward me, but his eyes rolled back into his head. "Roan!"

A soft smile lay inside his beard, but he lay lax like a dead man. Smears of blood covered his torso rather than his shirt. I glanced back behind him but couldn't see too far in the distance in the dimness of night. He'd left his belongings behind. Somewhere.

I held his face in my hands again. "Roan. Wake up. Tell me what's wrong."

Nothing but a shiver and the rapid pulse in his throat let me know he lived.

"Fucking hell." I grasped under his armpits and tugged. "You weigh a fucking ton!" I growled at him, tugging again. We made it halfway to the stoop before I had to stop for a breather.

A few more pats on his face didn't rouse him. Light shining out of the open doorway revealed his lips were dried and cracked.

I hopped up and grabbed a cup of water and cradling his

head in my lap a few feet from the stoop, I touched the cup to his lips. "Come on, big boy. Help a woman out, will ya?"

Water trickled between his lips, and his reflexes took over, his throat working to swallow.

Just a few sips, and I set the cup aside, ready to drag his ass across the ground again.

A half-hour later, the cup of water empty, most of which I'd gotten into him, we made it up the stoop and into the cabin. I slammed the door shut and latched it.

I eyed him on the floor, wracking my brain. Fever. Shivers and passed out.

First things first—I needed to get his temperature down. I dragged the medicine box from beneath the bed, grabbed two Tylenol, and set to work crushing them into a fine powder. While the medicine didn't dissolve fully in warm water, it came close enough for me to get some inside him.

He gagged at the first mouthful I poured between his lips and came to enough to try to turn his face away.

"Come on, Roan. Drink it—it's going to take down your fever. Okay?"

Another tip of the cup, and he swallowed.

Groaned.

"Just a bit more. You can do this—for me." I poured the rest between his parted lips, and he swallowed like a good boy. "There. Wasn't so bad, was it?"

He didn't answer. Didn't twitch an eyelid.

I grabbed the sat phone.

"He's burning up with fever, Mom."

"What? Who?" Mom murmured—and I realized I'd woken her up.

"Roan. He's burning up—what should I do?"

A few shuffling noises sounded in my ear. "It's Annie," Mom said—probably to Dad. It had to be close to midnight, but I'd been so caught up in writing, I hadn't realized the time. "Roan's at the homestead. Burning with fever."

"Annie?" Dad's voice came through the phone.

"Dad." Tears sprang to my eyes. "What should I do?"

"What are his symptoms?"

"I-I don't know." I stared down at Roan as he curled in on himself. "He went off into the bush a few days back, and just showed up, half-clothed and feverish. He's passed out, Dad."

"You're going to be okay, Annie. Get the medicine box—"

"I already got two Tylenol in him."

"Good girl."

I tore the blanket off the bed and tucked it around his shivering form stretched out on the floor.

"It could be tularemia, so let's play it safe."

"Doxycycline," I whispered.

"Yes. There's two bottles of it there."

"Okay." I rummaged and found one. "Can I crush it up?"

"No. Wait for the Tylenol to kick in, and when he's lucid, give him the first dose, okay?"

"Okay."

I sat cross legged beside Roan, hating the feeling of helplessness. Hating that I hadn't been strong enough for him when he needed me, that I'd had to call my parents.

"Are you okay, baby girl?"

"Yes. I'll be fine," I stated a little louder, my sure tone giving me a boost of confidence.

"Want me to fly out there right now? I will if you need me to."

"No." Resolve settled in my gut. *I've got this. I can be strong for Roan, too.* "We'll be fine—and I'll call in the morning."

I hung up a few minutes later after more words of assurance and looked around the cabin. "You can do this, Annie."

Setting aside the cup and bottle of pills, I decided on a course of action. A plan. Roan needed a pillow since there was no way in hell I could get him into the bed on my own.

Once one of the two pillows lay beneath his head, I removed the blanket from his body, muttering at myself for covering him in the first place. The Tylenol would take twenty or so minutes to kick in, but I could help his body by cooling it down, too.

I grabbed the bucket of water off the counter and a rag. Sponge bath it would be since he sure as hell needed one anyway.

He must not have washed up since leaving. Dirt and smeared blood from his face and beard turned the water murky, the worst being the left side of his face like he'd lain in the dust, face-down for a few hours. Even his beard needed a thorough washing.

A serious clean up would have to wait, but I did what I could.

I wiped down his chest and arms, appreciating the cut, lean muscles of his torso and shoulders. A hard body shivering without control, though, dented my forehead with a frown. My chest ached to hold him close, warm him so he wouldn't shake like a leaf buffered by wind.

He groaned a few times, but didn't move, and I offered him more water—of which he drank down voluntarily.

"Roan?"

"Hmm..." He didn't open his eyes, but I continued to wipe down his belly, my fingertips trailing over the ridges of his ab muscles while wiping them clean of blood.

A raging fever, and his cock pressed against the zipper of his pants.

"Are you ready to wake up?" I asked, wringing out the rag again, determined to ignore his hardness and the arousal that dampened my panties at seeing him aroused from my touch even while burning with fever. The man seriously needed to get laid.

Had he ever had a woman?

"I want to get you into bed."

His lips twitched, and relief flooded through me even though he still shivered, still burned.

My belly fluttered as I bit back my own smirk. "You know damn well what I meant," I attempted to snip the words.

I wiped along his neck again, down over his shoulder, and refrained from trailing farther south over those washboard abs and that luscious V disappearing into the band of his pants.

"Roan?"

"Hmm." One eyelid twitched, allowing me a glimpse of green.

Thank fuck.

"How are you feeling?"

"Shit."

"Think you can help me get you up onto the bed? I can't do it on my own."

"Mmm hmm."

I set the rag aside and crawled to his feet. "Going to take off your boots first."

One of the laces hadn't been tied, and I slipped off that boot easily. The second had a knot all twisted to hell. I cut the damn thing with scissors after breaking one of my already short fingernails in an attempt to get it loose.

"I'll buy you new ones," I muttered and snipped. Tossing the other boot aside, I glanced up to find both of Roan's eyes open. Barely, but still. I smiled and moved closer to his head, placing my palm on his forehead. "Hey."

He swallowed. "H-hey."

"Ready to get up on that bed?"

"Mmm."

I helped him roll to his side, and he pushed up onto his hands and knees, letting out a groaned curse.

"Come on. I got you." I grasped under one arm and helped lift him up onto his knees.

Roan grimaced and clutched at the bedstead, his knuckles white.

"Almost there," I whispered, smoothing his hair back off his hot forehead. "That soft bed is going to feel like heaven. Just a bit more. You got this."

I held tight to his arm as he pushed up to his feet—and pitched forward to sprawl halfway on the bed.

My giggles and his groans accompanied our maneuvering him higher up and fully onto the bed until he rolled to his back with a deep sigh.

"Medicine time." I grabbed the antibiotics and a new cup of water. Propped on pillows, he had no problems taking the pill and emptying the cup. "The Tylenol is helping, and within forty-eight hours or so, the antibiotic will kick in, too."

I eyed his filthy pants, the blood-soaked knees. At least his cock seemed to have relaxed a bit.

"Want 'em off," he muttered.

The thought of Roan without pants set those butterflies to flight in my belly again. "I really should clean up your knees," I half-whispered another reason to strip him down, my heart rate jumping.

"M'kay." He fumbled with the pants clasp, and I realized his cut-up palms needed attention, too.

"You're a damn mess," I muttered, turning to grab the blanket off the floor.

He'd shoved his pants mid-thigh by the time I returned, and I caught an eyeful of that python, long and heavy, lying up over his hip bone. Not hard and leaking, but damn well on its way.

Holy fucking hell. I tossed the blanket over his groin, needing to hide that thing before drool dripped from my parted lips.

His eyelids had closed again, a slight furrow between his eyebrows, hands lax at his sides.

"I'll help," I murmured, yanking his pants to his ankles. No tighty whities. No boxers or briefs.

I would never be able to look at Roan again without thinking about the easy access he had to that monster my pussy pulsed for.

Clearing my throat, I lifted his feet one at a time, to rid his body of the pants. "There. Now let me clean up your hands, your knees, then you're going to drink some broth for me."

Roan didn't reply, but he'd stopped shivering.

The pants hadn't ripped too badly at the knees, but enough that rocks had dug into his tender skin.

"What'd you do? Crawl down the mountain?"

He grunted.

"That desperate to get down here?"

"To you," he croaked.

My heart stalled out and kicked back in, but I focused on my work of cleaning up his knees rather than check to see if he stared at me. "They're not too bad. You don't even need bandages."

I made even quicker work of his hands and grabbed a box of beef bone broth from one of the crates behind the door.

"Too much of a pussy to drink it room temp?" I asked, reaching for a mug.

He grunted again, but I couldn't figure out what he'd meant. It didn't matter, though, what he wanted. I wasn't about to light a damn fire with the heat already filling the cabin.

I pushed the windows open all the way, hoping for a cross breeze, and pulled one of the chairs close to the bed.

Roan still lay propped up on the two pillows, arms drooped at his sides, powerful thighs and those abs covered by the blanket I'd tossed over him.

"Cold?"

"Uh uh."

A quick check with the digital thermometer let me know the Tylenol had lowered his fever where it wouldn't be dangerous.

"Here." I cracked open the box's top and poured some broth into a cup. "Let's get this into you, then I'll let you sleep."

I ended up cleaning a few dribbles from his beard, but Roan didn't complain or grumble about the broth's taste or temperature.

"Okay?"

A shiver spasmed his body, and I spread out the blanket better, tucking it around his chest.

He appeared to sleep, so I didn't speak, just cleaned up a bit before returning to his side.

I chewed the inside of my lip, wondering if I ought to sit by him, go back to Dad's comfy chair and try to write some more, or crawl up into the loft and get some rest. No way in hell I'd be able to focus on writing, and the thought of going up the ladder and leaving him alone didn't sit well with me. The hard chair I sat on certainly wouldn't do, either.

I dragged Dad's comfy one over beside the bed, crawled up to the loft to retrieve a blanket from the chest Mom kept up there, and came back down, settling in on my side, the chair kicked back to recline as far as it would go.

The fact Roan's fever had come down so easily soothed my worry and made me feel more confident. As long as I kept medicine in him, continued to give him the antibiotic, he would be fine. We wouldn't need Dad to fly Roan to a hospital, something I felt sure Roan would fight like a rabid hare, anyway.

I let out a heavy sigh and closed my eyes, the image of his dark lashes and parted lips burned into my mind.

Everything is going to be just fine.

ANNIE

R oan let out a groan, and I jerked upright, my blanket falling to my waist.

I'd left the lamp on, and a quick glance showed him shivering, his body twitching with chills.

"Shit." I hopped off Dad's chair and quickly smashed more Tylenol and mixed it in some water.

"Ann…" He groaned again.

"Almost ready, Roan. Hang in there," I murmured, swirling the water with a spoon. Good enough.

I returned to his side to find the blanket pushed low on his hips. Shivers rippled over him, and a deep frown dented his brow.

"Here," I whispered, sliding my hand beneath his head to lift him a bit. "Drink."

Roan turned his head toward me, breathing deeply. "Annie."

"I'm right here. Drink." I put the rim of the cup to his lips, but he didn't respond. "Come on, Roan. You need to drink this."

Another shiver jerked his body, loosening my hold on his

neck and nearly making me spill the Tylenol-laced water.

"Damnit. Come on."

His lips had parted, so I drizzled the liquid in, giving him time to choke a little down at a time.

He'd passed out cold again. No twitch of the eye, no frown.

I managed to get the rest of the medicine in him and settled back into my chair.

Sleep claimed me after what seemed eye-stinging hours.

Another deeply rumbled groan pulled me awake.

Roan had rolled onto his side, facing the wall. The blanket had slid low on his upper thigh, revealing his entire backside.

I stared for a few second, blinking the sleep from my eyes.

He shivered and shook, letting out another groan that sounded a lot like my name.

"Can't…" He murmured a few more incoherent words.

"Roan?" I lightly touched his back.

Burning up. A few more jumbled bits of nonsense muttered into the stillness.

Fucking hell.

He tried to speak, or did, rather, but made no sense.

Fuck!

I used all my strength to roll him toward me, knowing he hallucinated, and he latched onto my wrist with a grip tight enough I grimaced—but my gaze landed on his other hand.

He grasped the base of his very stiff, very fucking large cock.

Oh, dear Lord up in heaven. "Roan." I tore my attention

off the hand he squeezed himself with to look him full in the face as heat rushed through me clear to my damn toes.

Eyes closed. Deeply grooved forehead. He murmured my name, pulling me closer.

"Roan. Wake up." My voice didn't come out stern like I'd hoped for.

His hand moved in my periphery—along with his damn hips.

Holy hell, he's jerking off while burning the fuck up!

"Roan." I patted his face with my free hand, and he turned into my touch, nuzzling my palm with his mouth.

"Want…" he whispered.

A swift yank on my arm brought me down atop him, my t-shirt askew between us, his face in my neck. "Roan, what are you doing?"

"Mine." Hot breath caressed my neck. His whiskers tickled. He released my wrist and tangled his fist in my hair before I could shimmy off him.

"Roan. Let go."

His other hand bumped into my knee as he jacked his cock.

Heat swept over me like a damn swell of flame, burning me from the inside out. He let out another groan, his lips nuzzling my neck.

Rather than push away, I swallowed and wet my lower lip as all the moisture in my body rushed between my thighs. "Roan." I grasped his hand in my hair, trying to pry his fingers loose.

"Sweet…my Annie."

The heat of his belly against mine worried my brain even as the hard muscle, the hand pulling on my long tresses, the moist warmth of his breath on my neck swayed my body to impale myself on the length he continued to work.

I should have pushed away.

I should have punched him rather than release his hand tangled in my hair and clutch at the pillows alongside his head.

I should have kneed him in the balls.

"Roan, let me go." My damn voice shook, from arousal rather than fear, and I didn't know what the fuck to do.

"Annie." He rolled toward the wall, pinning me to the bed beneath him before I could decide.

My heart stalled out—and burst with a shot of adrenaline.

Roan's burning body weighed me into the mattress, his shivering, shifting muscles working fast enough to grasp my wrists overhead before I could fight him off.

"Roan," I whispered even as wetness soaked through my panties. "Roan, you need to wake up. Please."

He continued to nuzzle my neck, the weight of him making it hard for me to breathe.

"R-Roan…"

A shift of his torso settled him between my thighs—damn thighs I should have pressed tightly together. Legs I should have been kicking with but didn't.

I stilled at the feel of his hardness along my inner thigh and told myself I couldn't fight him because he was sick. He didn't know what he was doing. I didn't want to hurt him.

Roan thrust his hips, grinding his cock along my leg. A smear of pre-cum eased his second thrust.

Okay…so let him blow his load against my leg while hallucinating. He won't remember in the morning—no biggie.

The groan against my neck clenched my eyes shut, and my hips tried to lift as he ground against me again.

Fuck. He needed to stop before—

A full-on body shiver shifted him over my body, hot skin, taunt muscle…*fuck*, did he feel good.

He grasped my wrists in one of his big hands, reaching between us with the other. His fingers fumbled with my panties.

"Roan," I let out a ragged whisper—and he yanked the fucking things free.

Oh shit. Oh shit.

The backs of his knuckles brushed against my soaked lips. So damn wet—so damn needy.

He groaned and rubbed his knuckles along my core again.

I didn't *want* to be needy. I clenched my eyes shut as he shifted again, bringing the blunt head of his massive dick against my core. I held my breath and told myself to fight him, to deny what he would take without knowing.

He'd promised.

He'd—

One thrust shoved that massive thing halfway into my body, and I shrieked, my muscles tensing even as my pussy pulsed around him. "Oh, holy fucking God, Roan! Shit. T-too much! Too much."

He pulled out, my slick channel coating his length. Another thrust slid me along the bed, his cock stretching me, filling me to the point I couldn't breathe.

Fuck. Too big. Too fucking big.

Another drag out, another violent snap of his hips, and he slammed into my cervix, letting out a ragged whimper against my neck.

He held still. Shivered. All his weight pressing against me.

Whimpering, I shifted beneath him, trying to adjust to his length, his girth. Lifting my knees helped slightly—

A muttered curse came out hot against my neck, and Roan's muscles tensed, dragging his dick out again.

Oh. Fuck…yes. My body attempted to arch beneath him,

chasing the massive cock backing away from me even as I lied to myself that I didn't want it.

"D-don't stop. Don't…Roan." I clasped my ankles around his ass and tried to pull him back to me, but he pulled out entirely, the head of his cock resting against my pulsing pussy, not even notched. A kiss of wet skin, teasing. Aching and throbbing for more.

A shudder rippled over him. "Mine," he growled and thrust, stealing my breath again, shattering all my thoughts.

Whatever he hallucinated, whatever he imagined doing, it was ten times more than I expected a virgin man of the wilderness would know. He moved with instinct, fucking into me with deep thrusts, grinding his pelvis against my clit as though trying to weasel in deeper—like he wanted to breach my cervix and make himself at home deep inside my womb.

The ache, the stretch, the luscious burn of him—he lit me on fire. Rushed heat from my fingertips still held in his strong grasp over my head to my toes, curling in attempts to keep him closer.

He took, and my body responded, my brain shut off. Shut down. Living my fantasy…

I fought to rise beneath his weight to meet him, my hips squirming to keep him rubbing against my throbbing clit.

Roan panted and gasped, finally releasing my hands to lift somewhat onto his elbows allowing me to breathe. Head hanging, hot forehead rubbing along my damp brow with every thrust deep inside me.

Sweat rose between us, our bodies slick and sliding, his fever bringing on one inside me to the point I felt near combustion.

"Roan. P-please."

He slid his hands beneath my back and clutched at my

shoulders, jerking my body downward along the mattress to meet his thrusts.

So deep. So hard—fucking Roan Kelly ruined me for life. No cock, no muscled body, no heated or soft skin, would ever compare.

I came without warning, shrieking his name, my thighs holding him tight, my fingers clasping at the hard muscle lining his spine.

He thrust once…twice…and wet heat erupted inside me, a mixture of grunts, groans, and whimpers accompanying his sporadic movements.

A big O at the same time.

Tingles raced over my shivering skin. Un-fucking believable.

My brain caught up to my panting body, and I lay beneath him, his body coming to rest on me like a corpse.

Dead, fucking weight.

I shimmied my torso to the side enough I could breathe, but his cock stayed lodged deep inside me, his upper body pressing on half of mine, smothering one of my boobs.

"Heavy fucker." I groaned and tried to push him off me. No such fucking luck. "Shit." I relaxed and smoothed my hair out of my eyes, lifting my head to see what to do.

Roan's biteable ass lay between my lax thighs, his hairy legs stretching clear to the end of the bed.

I smoothed a hand down his back, my forehead furrowing at the heat of his skin.

I need to get some meds in him.

Lips in a thin line, I pushed—fucking shoved at his hips with my legs and thighs, slowly easing his thick cock out of my body. With complete release, a rush of wetness seeped from my core.

"Shit, Roan." I slithered the rest of the way out from

under him, leaving him lying face down, his groin in our combined cum. "You're lucky I'm about to start my period any day now," I muttered, wondering if the cramps inside me came from its start or Roan's cock jabbing me half to death.

Refusing to think any more on what he—*we* had done—I cleaned up, my legs shaky as well. I crushed up a pill and put it in water, my hands no less unsteady.

He hadn't moved, but still lay like the dead. At least he didn't shiver.

A hand on his back revealed he still burned up, though.

"Okay, python. Time to roll back this way and take your medicine." I set the cup on the bed stand, got onto my knees on the edge of the bed, and grasped his hip and shoulder. "Roan," I called out loudly, "you need to roll your big ass over, you hear me?"

He didn't budge.

"Come on you fucking lug!" I yanked, but barely got his shoulder off the mattress.

Fuming, I stared at the back of his damn head—shaggy hair needed a good cut.

"Roan!"

Nothing.

"Goddamn you to fucking hell." I yanked a few more times, my eyes starting to sting with frustration. "How the fuck am I supposed to get this fucking medicine in you!"

I pinched his ass, and he flinched.

I pinched again— harder, and he groaned.

"Let's go. Onto your back."

I smacked his ass, and he ground his hips against the bed. Eyebrow raised, I considered my scarred palm and the slight red print blooming on his ass cheek. I let loose with another smack, telling myself he deserved it.

My lips smirked as he thrust against the bed again. "You

kinky fucker." I glanced down at his feet, and my smirk spread out full on my face. Scooting to the bed's end, I made sure to keep from of his limbs—just in case.

Trailing a fingertip up his arch, I watched the back of his head like a damn hawk.

"Roan," I whispered loudly. "There's a huge spider on your foot."

His leg twitched, and I lightly scraped my fingernail along his arch again.

"Spider, Roan."

He groaned and shifted, lifting his knee to escape the "spider".

Another light touch got him onto his side, knees curling up toward his chest.

Rather than take a chance of him lashing out, I crawled up between him and the wall, planted my feet against the smoothed lumber for leverage and pushed my shoulder into his.

He rolled onto his back with an oomph noise.

I grabbed the blanket and threw it over his cock before temptation to get another good look won out since just thinking about how he'd stretched me made me wet and ready for another round.

Five minutes later, I had the Tylenol in him, our cum wiped up off the sheet, and he seemed to rest quietly.

Refusing to dwell on what had happened, I stretched out Dad's chair again and snuggled on my side beneath the other blanket.

A sweet sting, an ache throbbed between my thighs, but I couldn't find it in myself to hate him. He hadn't been fully conscious—and it'd felt too damn good.

Too big.

Too damn good.

15

ROAN

A clinking sound dragged my eyelids open.

I blinked, bringing a log ceiling into focus. The scent of coffee hit my nose, and I let out a groan, turning my head.

Annie eyed me from the kitchen area, the coffee pot in her hand.

I made it to her. Made it to the cabin.

Licking my dry lips, I closed my eyes again.

Soft bed. Warm blanket.

My body ached, my head throbbed, but I lived.

A soft palm caressed over my forehead, just like Ma's had done when I'd been a child. I leaned into the touch, a sigh settling over me.

"How are you feeling?"

My sweet Annie… No snark in her tone.

I cracked open an eyelid again. Her dark eyes peered down at me, but exhaustion kept me from trying to see inside her.

"Like shit," I managed.

Lips tight, she nodded. "Can you scoot up a bit so I can help you drink some water?"

Water—fucking yes. I dug my heels into the bed and pushed, using my elbows to prop myself up a bit for the pillows she shoved behind my neck and head.

Annie didn't meet my gaze while holding the cup to my lips, but the second the water trickled in, I closed my eyes.

Hell, yes.

I drank down the whole glass.

"More."

She obliged, then set the empty glass aside.

"Tularemia," I muttered, closing my eyes, and resting again.

"That's what my Dad thinks, too." Her voice sounded distant like she'd moved away.

"He here?" I forced my eyes open, but they slipped closed just as fast after seeing her pouring coffee.

"No. I called him right before I made the coffee. Your fever broke, so we agreed to see how you fared after forty-eight hours of antibiotics. I figured you wouldn't want to be flown out of here to a hospital unless I couldn't get the fever down."

She'd figured right. "How many doses did you get into me?"

"One last night—and I managed another about an hour ago. Been crushing up Tylenol in water. Had a few doses overnight."

I could sense her moving close again.

"Want to try some coffee?"

"No."

She sat in silence, and I dozed. Drifted—but not in blackness like before. Memories of crawling toward the cabin filtered through my brain as I rested. I remembered Annie pulling me toward the light.

"How'd you get me up here on the bed?" I muttered, eyes still closed.

"You were on the floor for a while at first. The Tylenol helped that you came to enough to help me get you up there."

"Mmm." I flexed my hands, my arms. Legs and feet. Testing to see how much I really hurt. "I'm not wearing pants."

Annie shifted on her Dad's chair she'd set beside the bed. "No."

I forced my eyelids up at her wary tone. "Did I take them off?"

Red fused her cheeks, and she glanced away. "We, uh… both did."

"Did my dick behave?" I whispered with a smirk as my eyes shut again. "Can't imagine he wanted to being bared to you and all."

Annie didn't answer, and my lips eventually leveled out again as I drifted. My Annie. Smelled so sweet. So soft and…wet.

My mind stilled as awareness settled over my brain, and I turned my head to find her peering intently at me. "I-I think I dreamed about you." My brow furrowed as I tried to bring it back. "Us," I whispered and swallowed, the dream wavering into memory.

Her dark eyes pinned me in place, her cheeks no longer pink. "It was no dream, Roan."

Fuck. I swallowed hard but refused to look away like a coward. "I'm sorry," I rasped out. "So fucking sorry, Annie."

She didn't frown, didn't smile. "You were hallucinating. Burning up with fever and didn't know what you were doing."

"That's no excuse." I scowled, my hands itching to reach for her, to make things okay between us. I'd fucked Annie—I could fucking remember her tight body allowing me inside. Wet heat. Snug and fucking perfect. My dick twitched, and I clenched my eyelids shut and teeth tight.

"Put that python away."

"Python?" My eyes shot open to find hers less troubled than a moment earlier.

She motioned at the tented blanket over my hips.

"Shit." I pressed down against my length, trapping my hard-on to my thigh. "Why do you call it that?"

"Because it's so…huge."

I couldn't help my smug grin, while studying her bland face. "Really?"

Her nipples pebbled and pulse thrummed in her neck. "I could feel you in the back of my throat," Annie muttered as though unhappy over that fact.

My dick jerked in my hand at her words, and I bit back a groan, willing my hard-on away. "Please tell me I didn't hurt you. I didn't, did I?" I asked through clenched teeth, trying to ignore the fact her body suggested she might want what throbbed in my hand.

"No," she whispered, holding my gaze. Lips thinning as though pissed, she picked up her coffee and left me in my corner of the cabin.

My stomach twisted all the same. "Did you fight me, Annie? Tell me to stop and I didn't?"

"I didn't fight."

She let *me take her.*

"Did it feel good?" I asked on a whisper, not for my ego, but desperate to hear she'd enjoyed it, didn't hate me for it— wouldn't fuckin' hold it against me.

Annie paused, her back stiffening, but didn't turn. "I didn't fight, but I didn't *want* it."

A wave of guilt slammed into me, taking out my hard-on, and I closed my eyes, wishing I'd died out beneath the stars.

I had taken when I'd promised not to. Even if she had fought against me, I doubted my control in the moment. Hell, I could barely remember much beyond softness and wet warmth.

My dick twitched at the memory, but I grimaced it away, focusing on the sting in my palms and knees instead. On the fact I hadn't been man enough to control my instinctive urges to mate with her.

"So, so fuckin' sorry, Annie," I whispered.

I lay there and soaked and wallowed in my guilt, knowing I'd hurt her—not physically, but hurt all the same.

She didn't accept my apology. She didn't speak a word.

The sound of her typing away at her keyboard lulled me to sleep after what seemed forever.

16

ANNIE

Forty-eight hours on the antibiotic, and his fever stayed only slightly elevated. Enough I assured my parents he would heal up just fine. He drank plenty of water, came close to wiping out my bone broth supply, and nibbled on sourdough biscuits I decided to make.

Lighting the wood stove had heated the cabin to unbearable, so I kept the windows and door propped wide open.

In late afternoon, I suggested Roan try to get up a bit and move around. He'd become restless atop the bed, bored, I expected, since I all but refused to talk to him, speak of what had happened.

Bottling up my emotions certainly didn't help, but I didn't know what to think or how to feel.

I wanted him again. I wanted to hate him. Being with Roan didn't fit into the goals of my life—no man did.

I tossed him a pair of sweats of Dads from the bin of extra clothes up in the loft I'd taken to sleeping in, turned my back, and let him handle covering up his body I'd been dreaming about. The body I'd become feverish over and cursed myself for.

The ache remained between my thighs, but for more, not because of his rough taking. I'd given in and thrummed my clit the night before, straining to listen to his breath, heavy with sleep while I bit my lip to keep from groaning his name while coming.

He woke that morning rolled toward the wall, and I fought to keep my gaze from flitting toward him when he rolled to his back with a groan, offering a glimpse of rippled abs and tented blanket.

Damn him for ruining me. Making me crave what rarely lay relaxed between his thighs. Damn him even more for making me want something that put *me* on the back burner.

A part of me felt sorry for his ass, being trapped up in the cabin with me, both of us silent beyond necessity, the sexual tension and unease heavy in the air. He probably ached for release as much as I did for him.

"Ready to get out of here?" I asked, my back still toward him.

"Yeah."

I turned to find he'd already sat up on the bed's edge by himself, something I'd had to help him do a few times in the past couple of days to empty his bladder in the old bed pan Mom kept beneath the bed.

Lips tight, I ignored his bare upper body, stepped to his side, and pulled his arm over my shoulders. "Up you go, big boy."

He stood easily, but stayed planted by the bed's side, the heat of him against my entire side fluttering my belly and intensifying that empty feeling deep inside me.

"You okay?" I asked, my voice tight.

"Yeah. Need a fuckin' bath."

I snickered, having to agree, but I doubted he'd make it all the way down to the river. "We could try getting you down to the river," I suggested as he shuffled a few feet toward the open door.

He grunted a negative. "I'll just wash up again with the bucket before bed."

We made it to the threshold, and Roan grasped the doorjamb with one hand. I'd already set one of the chairs outside beneath the overcast sky, figuring if he sat on the stoop he might not have the energy to get back up.

Once settled, I eyed his bare feet and the dust clinging to him from our short walk on the packed earth.

"Definitely need a good washing. I can fill up Mom's small tub if you want."

"You're not lugging water all the way up here."

"I'll do it if you want me to."

Roan studied me, his green eyes completely clear of fever since I'd dragged his big ass inside the cabin. "I'm sorry," he whispered.

"I don't want to talk about it."

"I do."

"Well, I don't," I snapped, staring out over the hills rising behind the house. "It's in the past, same as that stolen kiss, so let's just leave it there."

Roan let out a heavy exhale. "Will you read your book to me?"

My focus jerked his way, and although his eyes held no evidence of teasing or manipulation, I wondered over his intent. I wouldn't be swayed into letting my guard down just so he could get what he wanted from me.

"Please, Annie. You always told the best stories—and I'm fuckin' bored. Need help escaping my mind."

His mind or his libido?

Biting back a smirk because of course I had to go there

and think like a bitch, I stood from my perch on the stoop. "I wrote a really hot sex scene last night. I could read you that."

He groaned as I hurried into the cabin to get my computer. "Fuck, no, Annie. Keep it tame. I'm barely able to think past my aching balls as it is."

Snickering to myself, I settled back on the perch, my heart rate amped up a bit. I knew I wrote good stories. I knew the second book I'd been working on would give him the escape he wanted. But a part of me flushed with embarrassment, with the tiniest bit of self-doubt and insecurity that came from so many people brushing off my dreams as being silly.

Roan's own brow had furrowed like he wondered what the fuck I was thinking when I'd told him about my dreams.

Well, fuck him if he didn't like my story. Fuck him if he thought my reading out loud, and his lying over loving it would get him between my thighs again.

Bitch Annie did what she did best—told her story to the man who sat in the chair with his eyes closed, a soft smile on his lips—with zero intention of letting him take from her again.

17

ROAN

Annie had written a story unlike anything I'd ever read. Including those romance novels her mom brought out for my sisters. The inner turmoil of the characters came alive inside me, twisting my guts up as fate brought them together with a crash—literally. Two cars, head on. One spouse dead, one living with guilt and remorse even though she hadn't been at fault.

Two broken souls meeting again a year later, one still haunted by causing a death, the other healing through grief therapy.

Eventually friends, then turning into lovers.

An unexpected pregnancy—blame coming about because of misunderstood intent when there'd been no attempt to manipulate.

Annie's voice had grown hoarse by the time she neared the end of the first book, heading toward a cliff hanger ending she'd warned me about.

We'd gone inside, ate peanut butter biscuits and apples for dinner, and I sprawled on my belly on the bed, my arms beneath the pillow, my focus on her face as she'd read from her dad's chair beside me.

She whispered *the end*, and paused, her focus still on her screen, working her lower lip between her teeth.

My dick had swelled at the first sex scene an hour or so earlier—the reason I laid on my stomach—and the sight of her biting her lip drew my balls up, pre-cum leaking.

I needed to empty the fuckers but had no way to hide the evidence. What I needed was to get my ass out to the outhouse so I could ease the pent-up desire I'd been fighting since releasing inside her body.

"You left me hanging," I whispered raggedly, with more than one meaning on my mind.

Pink tinted her cheeks, a smile twitching her lips as she finally released her teeth's hold on the lower. Reddened and plumped from her biting, they held my stare. Sent another ache through my groin.

Had I kissed her while rutting mindlessly between her thighs? I couldn't remember. Couldn't remember tasting her skin or how she felt beneath my hands.

Fuck. Did I even touch her beyond shoving my dick inside her?

And I'd asked if she'd enjoyed it.

Fuckin' bastard.

"Hey."

I lifted my gaze to find Annie peering down at me.

"You okay?" she asked, her voice quiet.

Her insecurities shone clear through her eyes, and I swallowed against the sudden crash of guilt knifing at my chest. "I'm sorry."

She rolled her eyes and climbed off her dad's chair.

"The story was really good," I called after her as she shuffled toward the table she kept her writing stuff on. She didn't reply but went about plugging her computer into the battery pack charger thing, same as she'd done the night before.

Without a word, she turned down the lamp and climbed the ladder to the loft, leaving me in the dark, wondering after her mind, her heart.

That damn guilt kept me awake long after my relentless hard-on eased enough I could relax.

———

The next afternoon, I shuffled down to the river, Annie at my side in case I needed help. I made it on my own, feeling a shit ton better than the day before. She left me alone with a towel and bar of soap, and I got to work, scrubbing the dirt from my entire body—and finally fuckin' relieving myself even though the water was cold as fuck.

Didn't shrivel my balls or my dick until long after I'd emptied them.

Finally clean, I dried off and pulled back on the other pair of pants her father kept in the emergency bin in the loft. They were a bit short, but only slightly tight in the thighs and ass. Cradled my dick a bit snug, and I knew I'd be in trouble come a few hours when my balls built up another supply of cum.

But I'd be able to make use of the outhouse on my own.

No more need to worry about hiding evidence of what she did to me, how the memory of her tightness choked my girth.

Annie sat halfway up the pebbled path waiting for me to finish, arms wrapped around her upturned knees. Her slow gaze down over my bare chest, to my unlaced boots, and back up, fluttered my stomach. At least my dick didn't twitch. Not even when I drew closer and saw the throbbing pulse in her neck and the beaded nipples pressing against her shirt when she stood.

"Feel better?" she asked, her tone guarded as it had been since she'd asked me that morning if I wanted coffee.

"Much."

"I'll wash out your pants," she murmured, ambling along at my side as we made for the cabin. "Dad's can't be too comfortable."

"A little tight, but they'll do."

Annie checked in with her dad a little later, and he let her know a storm headed our way, finally bringing some rain to the dried-out land around us. We had a bit of time before it arrived, and even though darkness and the scent of rain already filled the sky, we washed out my pants and socks together, hanging them inside the cabin to dry.

She made a stew of canned meat, rice, and greens from the tiny garden she'd watered and cared for since arriving on the homestead, and we ate outside, sitting on the stoop to escape the cabin's heat.

Sweat beaded both our brows while we washed up the dishes.

A welcomed breeze rushed through the house suddenly, and both of us let out a groaned sigh.

"Finally," she muttered, wiping her forearm over her face.

Flushed, a sheen of sweat on her forehead, she looked like a ripe berry ready to be devoured.

Damn dick took note, but I turned away and stood in the open doorway, waiting for the thickening to relent. Fuckin' thing didn't, and I clenched my teeth, knowing it was time to go.

Annie didn't want my apologies. Didn't want to discuss what had happened between us. She wanted to forget about it, and the sooner I got out of her hair, the sooner she would accomplish what she'd come to the homestead to do.

The sooner she could move on her life, while I wallowed in guilt and unhappiness.

"Think you'll finish sooner than September?" I asked without turning, eyeing the storm clouds rolling in the distance.

"Yes," she didn't hesitate to reply. A goshawk soaring confidently toward her dreams.

My almost-smile faded as the fact she preferred flying alone crashed against me. "I'm going to head home tomorrow."

Annie didn't reply, but I felt her gaze on my back as real as her palm on my forehead that morning checking for fever.

Thunder rumbled in the distance, but the storm took its good old time. Lightning flashed over the mountains, the crackling and booming chasing its heels.

We left the windows open when crawling into our beds, but I expected once the skies let loose, we'd have to shut them up against the downpour promised by the looming clouds.

18

ANNIE

I laid in the sweltering heat, waiting for the storm slowly rolling our way to finally sweep in and cool off the air like Dad promised over the phone earlier in the afternoon. Finally, a cooler air front moving down from the north. I couldn't wait.

A hot breeze occasionally flitted over my bare skin with every distant rumble of thunder. Being out of sight of the bed beneath the loft, I decided to sleep in only my panties, too damn hot to consider anything else.

Heat prickled my underarms and kept the feeling of constant sweat coating my skin. Deciding to stand out beneath the rain once it started, I kept my t-shirt close by.

I could hear Roan shifting on the bed beneath me between cracks of thunder, and similar restlessness kept me from sleep. I'd been antsy, more aroused than annoyed, reliving every moment he'd been on top of me, inside me. And the last thing I wanted was his apology. I didn't trust it, didn't trust him or his intentions in stating it over and over.

The continued apologies pissed me off.

He needed to let it go—even though my brain and body couldn't seem to.

He would leave in the morning, and I should have been happy at the prospect of having the cabin to myself once more. Peace and quiet. No rumbling voice pebbling my nipples. No bare chest, broad shoulders, and bulging sweatpants thrumming my heartbeat. No sexually charged energy filling up the cabin's small interior making my lungs feel like they couldn't draw enough oxygen to sustain my hungry body.

The storm grew closer, the unrest in the air matching my insides while waiting for the rain to start falling.

A bright flash lit the cabin's windows, jacking a rush of adrenaline through my blood with the thunder crashing almost atop it.

Shit, that was close.

I lay still, slowing my breath.

The hairs on my arm stood on end—and another boom shattered the night, shaking the cabin at the same time an explosion of light filled the interior. My ears rang, and I sat up, my skin tingling like I'd stuck my wet finger into a light socket.

"Annie?" Roan hollered as another boom of thunder actually shook the damn cabin.

I scrambled to tug on my t-shirt and scurried down the ladder, uncaring I only wore panties, and he might see up my shirt. While I wasn't scared of thunder and lightning, that had been too damn close.

Roan yanked up Dad's sweatpants that had been hanging to dry over the back of the chair beside his bed, his gaze on the window he crowded against.

An eerie orange glow lit his face.

Shit.

"Fire," he whispered and jerked around to grab his boots at the same time my brain shut down.

I stared at the window, could feel the heat rushing at me, stealing the oxygen from my lungs.

Fire. Searing pain.

"Annie!" Roan barked, blinking my focus on his face still lit from the light of the fire outside the cabin. "We have to go! Now!"

Still, I stared, my knees locked. Brain fried and shut down.

Roan grasped my hand and yanked me toward the front door, and I stumbled, reality crashing against the memory of another fire. Skin blistering heat and unbearable pain.

I yanked against his hold, clawing at his hand, desperate to flee, to escape him. "Let me go!"

"Annie!" he hollered atop another boom of thunder, and I spun toward Dad's chair, grabbing my computer—my life, my dreams. All my hard work.

I sobbed, choking for air, clutching the computer to my chest, and running toward the door he yanked open.

We stepped outside into a sky lit orange and red— sparks dancing high into the air, whipping on the wind blasting my face and hair with unbearable heat and soot.

Flames ate at the brush, flared along dried out lichen, racing from the hills toward the cabin like a roaring grizzly, intent on devouring everything.

Tears rolled down over my cheeks as Roan grasped my arm and yanked me toward the river. The raging fire crackled, the wind roared—and the damn sky lit with another crack of thunder.

Shrieking, I huddled my shoulders up near my ears,

clutching my damn MacBook like it could save me, a lifeline to safety—

Phone. Need the phone to call Dad.

I pulled up short, knowing I needed to get back to the cabin, but Roan held onto my arm with a death grip, dragging me down the pebbled path, one side of its brush already dancing with death's flames.

"The sat phone!" I hollered, pulling against his hold.

Fire arched through the air, its angry, flickering arms reaching, seeking out fuel across the path ahead of us.

With a growl, Roan pulled me up into his arms, jostling my hold on my computer.

"Roan!" I shrieked as my life, all my work, tumbled from my arms and bounced off the pebbled ground.

The fire howled, and he ducked through the wall of flame, bringing us out on the other side along the river's edge, his legs pumping, stumbling. He crushed me to his chest as I fought to free myself.

I needed the phone to call Dad. Needed my computer!

Roan had claimed to love my book, claimed to believe in me, but he left all my blood, sweat, and tears on the path behind us.

He didn't care.

He'd only been after one thing all along, just like I'd thought, lying to get between my thighs again—

He muttered something about touching and time against my hair, his arms like steel bands.

Sobbing, I writhed, wiggled, but he didn't loosen his hold on me.

"No time," he muttered over and over, his feet splashing in the river as he strode ever onward.

Water hit my legs as he moved forward. Cold water soaked my backside—my waist—as he continued moving into the current. I gave up my fight to escape and clung to the only anchor available.

"T-too deep!" My teeth chattered from the adrenaline lagging more than the water's chill.

Still, he moved toward the other side, the untouched land, free of fire and smoke.

Finally, he paused, the water at his chest, and I clung to him, my heart racing, my eyes bleeding tears.

"Too deep to cross," he stated, his voice cracking. Turning, we faced the fire.

Flames shot from the roof of the cabin, the heat of the burning land and log home reaching us in the river. Heat seemed to bake my face like a mid-summer's sun, hot, but with a promised kiss of death rather than enjoyable warmth.

Sobs ripped from my lips as I watched my family's summer home disappear behind a wall of wavering red, gold, and orange, black smoke swirling in the wind blowing northward rather than in our faces.

I clung to Roan, angling away from the fire, and wrapping my body around his, legs around his waist. Face in his neck, I fought to keep from completely losing my shit, sobbing, and gasping for breath from the occasional eddies of smoke that reached our way. Shivers attacked me, and I couldn't keep my teeth from clattering.

Too cold.

Too deep.

The pain too much.

Roan's feet lost traction against the rushing water swirling around us, and he stumbled, quickly righting himself, his arms holding me tighter.

"Annie."

I pulled back at the anguish in his tone and found tear

tracks washing away the soot clinging to his cheeks. Desolation wrecked his beautiful eyes. Fear. Regret.

"Annie." One arm clutched around my waist, he released the other to cradle my face in his wide palm. "I'm so sorry."

So was I—for so damn much, I couldn't even voice my pain.

ROAN

Bleak eyes set alight with the glow of the fire angrily licking up every dried-out twig, grass tuft, and tree in its path… I'd never seen anything so damn fragile—yet beautiful as Annie staring at me. No hope. No chance of escaping across the river to untouched land.

I'd promised to not take. I'd promised myself I wouldn't allow my instincts to rule—but knowing death awaited us, I had no choice.

A flash of lightning lit her beautiful face, and thunder boomed overhead, ringing my ears.

I needed to live. Needed to hold onto the rush of *life* in my veins until my heart stopped.

I crashed my mouth against hers, tears, soot, and snot be damned.

She clung to me, her sobs filling my mouth as I licked at her mouth. Tasting. Overwhelming need to devour, same as the hungry fire laying waste to the Charran homestead, crashed into both of us.

Annie grasped at my hair rather than punch at my back.

Tightened her legs around my waist rather than push away like I'd expected.

Despite the cold water, its steadily ripping current, the rage of deadly flames crackling, and howling wind filling my ears, my body tightened for her. Heated with the need to mate, to claim, before Mother Nature ended us.

Feet planted wide, I braced against the rushing water, but couldn't protect myself from the emotions slamming into me like a flash flood. The scent of fear, of sweat, couldn't erase the sweetness of my Annie. The surety of death by fire or drowning couldn't demolish my need for her.

"Not sorry," I told her, between lashes of our tongues. "Need you…you're *life* to me, Annie."

She rubbed against me as though frantic, bucking her hips, whimpering into my mouth while I licked and sucked, nibbled, and thrust my tongue deep into her.

Desperate. Because we stood at death's door.

My dick strained between us, uncaring of the cold, uncaring life could be ripped away with the next breath.

"Roan!" Annie cried out suddenly, jostling my memory of her having done it once before, her body shuddering in my arms as lightning struck again.

"Not. Sorry." I clutched her tighter, grinding my dick against her until my balls erupted in a rush of heat spurting inside the sweatpants between us.

Coming from kissing and rutting alone, adrenaline spiked in my blood beyond any I'd felt before.

We clung to one another, our breaths ragged, and I tucked Annie's head into my neck, cradling her to me, as the noise and flashes of the impending storm raged, as the wildfire devoured everything in front of me.

Eyes closing, I lifted my face to the sky, ready for it to be over.

I hadn't been inside her, but I'd never felt closer. Felt like she'd burrowed deep inside *me*.

"It's okay," I murmured. "It's okay."

Mother Nature could take me, the quicker the better. Annie had let me in. Clung to me like I was the only thing she needed, like I'd proven myself good enough. A mere chickadee allowed to soar the skies with its better…even if I had taken without asking.

"Not sorry," I whispered one last time.

The skies finally opened up, and heavy rain drops drenched my head in seconds.

I blinked through the pouring rain, taking a few steps closer to shore as the threat of singeing heat and death lessened. Slowly, the drenching rain smothered the raging fire as I stood in thigh-deep water, Annie's legs still wrapped tightly around my waist, my arms continuing to cradle her close.

Neither of us spoke.

The flames stood no chance of survival, same as I'd thought of us both Annie and me what seemed hours earlier.

I eventually stepped onto the pebbled shore, one boot somehow gone, standing, and staring as steam fought to rise from the burnt ground against the steady downpour. My knees gave out as exhaustion set in, and I sank to the ground, still holding Annie tight against my chest.

"Is it gone?" she whispered against my ear, her body shivering in my arms.

I couldn't see up the rise to the cabin from our low vantage point, but the imprinted image of fire eating at the logs answered her question the same as seeing the results.

"Yes. The cabin," I rasped, soothing my hand down her one arm in attempts to warm her, "and the fire."

She shuddered, quietly crying as the rain drops continued to pound on my head and shoulders, thumping on the blackened ground around us. No matter how I curled my body around hers, Annie continued to shiver.

I closed my eyes and simply existed. Somehow alive—and beyond grateful.

———

My legs cramped beneath us before the rain let up.

We found Annie's computer where I'd forced her to leave it behind, melted and ruined beyond repair, all her hard work, the long hours gone.

Tears slid down her cheeks as she picked it up, the soot blackening her hands.

I swallowed, fearing the sure hatred to come my way, but I couldn't be sorry. "Your life meant more to me than anything in that moment, Annie. Anything. I would have gladly tossed you into the river and been burned to ash myself if it had been the only way to save you."

She nodded without looking at me—more a resigned gesture than anything, leaving me floundering. Wondering over her emotions toward me.

I might have saved her life, but that didn't change the fact she didn't belong in my world.

The black clouds eased northward, their work of fighting what lightning had started competed. The burned down shell of the cabin smoldered, and Annie slipped her hand into mine as we stood a few feet from the stoop, peering over the home's remains.

Hope swelled inside me, and I wrapped my fingers tightly around hers, holding on with everything inside me.

"What are we going to do?" she whispered, sounding like a small child. Her hair hung tangled down her back, soaked, and clinging to her the same as the t-shirt to her skin, to the soft swells of her bare breasts beneath. Shoulders rounded, she tossed aside the computer she'd held in her other hand.

Tears rolled down her cheeks, and the dark eyes she lifted my way filled with the type of pain no amount of skin grafts or physical therapy could heal.

We had no food. No clothing or blankets.

No antibiotics.

No sat phone or old radio to call for help.

I kissed her temple, my thumb brushing over her trembling lower lip.

"Head upriver to my parents," I murmured our only hope. A three-day hike with nothing more than her shirt and panties, my pants and single boot.

She nodded, her gaze as bleak as the sky, same as the heaviness in my chest over our chances of surviving what lay ahead.

Being without medicine worried me more than the other things we lacked. The disease, unhindered by antibiotics, would return with force, I expected, before we would be able to make the three-day hike, which would take longer, I knew, without proper shoes.

But we'd survived the fire, the river. I would push on through exhaustion and fever, no matter how it might rage.

Annie had trusted me to keep her safe in the river, and didn't seem to hate me for choosing her life over her work—I refused to fail her, no matter how dismal our situation.

Rumbles of thunder still sounded in the distance, but far to the north. I hoped my parents' homestead got hit with rain before lightning or racing flames. Did I have a home to return to? Did my family survive the rapidly advancing fire the wind had swept their way?

We wouldn't know how far the fire had spread until we reached the land's burned edges.

I eyed the wilderness disappearing into the darkness of night and heavy clouds. Black. Everything black as the horizon, not a hint of light or hope to be found.

20

ANNIE

We managed to get a bit of sleep curled up together on the hard, burned earth, shivering while sharing body heat. The storm had brought the cooler weather my dad had promised, and knowing we had a few days' hike ahead of us, we rifled through the cabin's remains in the morning, managing to salvage a few cans of food and Dad's bone-handled knife.

Better than nothing.

While I faced northward, wanting to flee the burned rubble, Roan studied the path leading up into the hills—where fire hadn't touched.

"What are you thinking?" I asked, my voice rasped from crying a lifetime worth of tears and the bit of smoke I'd inhaled trying to escape the fire.

"I'm thinking my pack is up there somewhere."

I turned to gaze over the vast expanse, a hint of hope swelling in my chest. "How far did you go?"

"A few miles—ten at the most."

Did we conserve our energy and strike out with close to nothing? No way to start a fire? Not nearly enough clothing to keep us warm if the nighttime brought even colder temperatures?

I glanced up to find Roan's eyes hard with a determined glint.

"I'm heading up there—I'll only go far enough to be back by night fall."

My stomach clenched tight, tightening my throat. "You're not leaving me here all alone."

He glanced down at my feet. "You don't have shoes."

"You only have one," I shot back, snipping my words. Fear led me more than concern. Fear of fire breaking out from buried embers and flaring up again to consume me. Fear of not having him to lean on should I need him to save me again.

He studied me, the hardness fading to a swell of emotion I couldn't think about—didn't want to.

But what if we didn't survive? Did I want to breathe my last without things settled between us? Roan had held me in the river, kissed me as though death hovered over us like the black clouds, and I'd done the same, thought the same.

"You would choose my life over yours," I whispered up at him, as his words about burning to ash echoed in my head.

"Every time," he didn't hesitate to answer, naked truth of his words shining in his eyes.

"You really didn't think my work was silly, did you?"

A frown flitted over his brow. "Why would you think that?"

"Because everyone but my family thinks that."

"Annie, you're incredibly talented. And I'm going to do everything in my power to keep you safe." He swallowed as though troubled. "To get you out of here so you can rewrite those stories and become a bestselling author—even if I don't understand what that is or how you'll go about doing it. I just know you will."

I slipped my hand into his, my throat tight. No one but my parents had ever put me first and believed in me so whole-heartedly. "If you need forgiveness, you have it. And I'm sorry for being such a bitch, for blaming you for an accident that my teasing had caused."

"It wasn't your fault."

"Either way, it happened. It's in the past, and I'm still able to type, to write." I lifted my scarred hand and studied it. "If nothing else, I have a constant reminder of my first kiss—and it couldn't have been more perfect."

Roan pulled me into his arms and kissed me without asking, but he no longer needed permission as far as I was concerned. He'd shown his worth, his character, even better than my dad.

Perhaps there was hope for my future after all.

"Don't leave me behind," I whispered my two-fold thought. I didn't want him leaving my heart behind once we got to safety—and I didn't want him heading into the hills without me, either. "Please."

He didn't argue, and we started off without another word, our going slow due to a lack of shoes.

An hour up into the hills left us traveling on dried lichen and grasses untouched by fire. We found his shirt along the hiking trail he'd stuck to even in his delirium. His old red sweatshirt lay a few hundred yards farther along.

He donned the shirt and insisted I take the heavier sweatshirt.

A mile later, a sob caught in my throat at the sight of his backpack laying in the middle of the trail like he'd left it on purpose, as though Mother Nature had whispered to his subconscious, telling him to prepare for our future.

He built a fire using the flint and extra knife he kept in his pack while I sat far enough away the fear of flames didn't choke me. Together, we built a lean-to of pine boughs, and burrowed together beneath the damp blanket his waterproof backpack hadn't quite protected from the rain.

Exhaustion hovered over us as Roan held me close, his hard chest and thumping heart beneath my ear offering a sense of safety enough, I fell asleep.

———

I knew Mom and Dad would fly out to the homestead within a matter of days of not being able to reach me—but last we'd left it, I promised to call later in the week to update them on Roan's condition unless he took a turn for the worse.

Five days, I expected, before anyone came looking for us. We would be at the Kelly homestead by then.

Expecting no one to rescue us but our own grit and determination, I followed Roan's lead the next morning, heading back toward the burned-out land below, his spare pair of socks on my feet acting as a buffer between tender skin from our hike the day before and unforgiving land.

From a bird's eye view, the devastation below hit me hard.

Dad had bought the place with the cabin already settled, but the second-floor loft, the woodshed, the outhouse, the cache built against the hill—all gone. Nothing but blackened logs.

He would be heartbroken, as would Mom. They'd started their life together down there. Created two lives in the very bed I'd spent the previous couple of weeks sleeping on.

Gone.

Nothing but memories.

My throat tight, I traipsed after Roan, not even glancing at the cabin's remains as we passed.

We hadn't found his rifle or canteen, so we decided to stick to the river's shore since water's importance outshone an extra day's travel. Stone and wayward sticks dug into my feet, some sharp enough to bite through the woven fabric of his woolen socks. They were better than nothing, but hardly enough to keep me from having to take one gingerly step after another.

Slow going, it seemed we barely made progress.

Emotional exhaustion just as taxing as the hike weighed on me with the can of cold stew we'd broken into that morning for breakfast hardly enough to sustain energy.

One can of corn, one green beans—and one of olives lay in the backpack strapped to his shoulders. The only food we had, the last of which Roan wouldn't touch.

We'll soon go hungry, but we'll make it.

The strong shoulders, the determined strides of the man leading me wouldn't allow for anything else. His strength would be enough to see us both through.

21

ROAN

Our second night beneath the stars, Annie curled her small body around me, clinging to me like she needed me. I'd never felt more content in my life. I had her forgiveness, and the warmth of her, the softness of her pressing against my front as we lay facing one another… Fuckin' *life*. Perfection, except for the beginnings of a fever I could feel brewing deep inside me.

Too soon. Too fuckin' soon…

I clenched my eyes shut and slid my hand beneath my sweatshirt she wore, calloused palm soothing over her back.

Annie let out a sigh as a shudder rippled over her.

"Cold?" I murmured against her hair tickling my nose, pulling her tighter against me.

"No." Her hot breath wafted over my collar bone, dampening my skin between my beard and the neck of my shirt.

A shiver slid down to my groin.

She took note of my thickening length—the first my body attempted a hard-on since the fire—and moved against me with a slight shift of her hips.

"Annie," I warned as lust thick and compelling, tightened my groin.

Her hot tongue licked along my shirt's collar, and I groaned, my hand slipping down her back to grasp her ass covered by silky panties.

"Fuck," I groaned, tipping my head back to give her better access. Sucking my lower lip between my teeth, I lay tense as a fuckin' spring ready to snap as Annie nuzzled at me, suckled on my skin.

"You taste like home," she whispered, lifting her head to peer down at me.

"I want to taste *you*," I rasped out, my dick already leaking.

Her lips parted in the dim summer night, allowing me to still see her face with clarity. Pupils dilated. Pulse thrumming in her neck. "Where?" she whispered, her fingernails digging into my shoulders.

I reached between her plump cheeks beneath my hand, fingertips sliding along satin. "Here," I choked out, rubbing at the damp heat beneath my touch.

"Roan…" Another whisper—but not a no.

I rolled her onto her back, held her gaze, and slid the panties off her legs. She shivered but stared at me with lust and so much more simmering in her eyes as I scooted down to settle between her spread legs.

Arms wrapping around her smooth thighs, I finally looked at what she'd teased me with that day on the river's shore. What I'd taken without seeing—and couldn't fully remember the feel of.

Dark curls, the pinkest petals, like a dew-covered flower, and the musky scent of her filling my nose…

I groaned, my dick fuckin' throbbing against the ground

beneath me. Had to close my eyes and breathe her in before losing my damn mind.

"Can I kiss you?" I growled out my desire, praying she would agree.

Annie's hands tangled in my hair, and she pulled my head forward, her hips rising to meet my hungry mouth.

Fuckin' hell, the taste of her…musk and tanginess, better than any damn canned peach or candy bar. I licked at her folds, dipped my tongue into the hole dripping with more of her cream, her whimpers and sighs fuckin' fuel to the wildfire raging inside me.

Our gazes caught and held while I licked up through her folds, clear to the small, hardened nub hidden in her soft, springy curls.

"Roan," she whimpered my name as I flicked my tongue over her clit.

"Is it enjoyable?" I murmured, flicking again.

"Yes."

"Want me to kiss you some more?"

"Fuck, yes."

I latched onto her clit and suckled like she'd done to my neck, and she bucked her hips beneath me, eyes clenching shut, head tipping back.

My dick leaked—wanted fuckin' more.

"Annie," I groaned against her pussy, and she yanked on my hair, tugging me upward.

"Yes."

I propped on one hand, used the other to shove down my sweatpants, and palmed my throbbing dick. "I put this inside you, I'm going to come undone before filling you."

"We have all night." Dark eyes, luminous in the glint of the moon held me ensnared.

I set the head of my dick against her small hole, no

fuckin' clue how I'd fit without ripping her in two—but I'd done it before in a fevered haze of lust.

"Fuck, Annie." I pushed, the tight heat of her clasping around my dick's head. "You're so fuckin' tight…" My eyes rolled back, and I held still even as she clutched at my head, trying to yank me closer, her heels digging into my ass.

"Yes, Roan. Please—yes."

I sank into her with a deep groan, barely getting half of my dick inside her before her body resisted me. At least I didn't blow like I'd thought I would.

"Back out," she whispered, and I did as told, the wetness of her coating my length. A tug of her heels on my ass, and I obeyed her silent command, sliding in deeper, the way eased by her wetness.

Teeth clenched, I swore harshly, my balls tight and ready to explode.

"Take, Roan," Annie gasped, her back arching her perfect body toward mine.

Fuck.

I lowered against her, took her fuckin' mouth—took her fuckin' little pussy that belonged to me with a harsh snap forward of my hips. Growling like a damn bear, I rutted into her, gone to restraint, gone to anything but the need ripping up my spine, demanding I give her everything.

"Fill you," I grunted the half-thought raging through my head, thrusting so damn deep, I swore I felt her heartbeat in the tip of my dick. "My cum…want to see it dripping out of your body."

Annie shuddered, and I thrust harder—faster. Chasing her body sliding along the blanket.

"Fuckin' mine, Annie, girl. Always… Mine."

Her pussy clamped around my girth, a rush of wetness leaking around me. "Yes!" My sweet Annie cried out, convulsing beneath me, her fingernails her heels digging into me.

Never seen or heard such a perfect, fuckin' sight.

My balls erupted as I stared down at her, my heart gone along with the breath she'd stolen from me.

I sat back on my haunches as the second spurt of cum tore up through my dick, keeping her body tight against my groin. A few more pulses of my cum oozed cum out around my buried length as though I filled her so damn full it had no place to go.

A slight shift pulled me out a few inches, but I shoved back in, wishing for full light so I could see better. Fill my eyes fully with the beautiful sight of Annie Charran allowing me to own her body.

She shuddered and sighed, pulling my focus from where we were joined. I watched her face while rubbing my thumb up over her clit.

"Oh!" She gasped and bit her lip, and I repeated the action, adding in a tiny thrust of my still hard dick against her womb.

"Too much?"

"Never."

Gazes once more latched, I eased in and out of her with long, languid strokes until she panted, eventually leaning once more over her, my hair hanging in my eyes.

"Can I kiss you?"

"Where?" She smirked up at me, her hands smoothing back my messed strands, causing my hips to pause their slow fucking in and out of her.

"Everywhere," I murmured what I wanted, and she lifted her head, taking my mouth in answer.

22

ANNIE

I slept the night through and woke in the morning, stiff and aching from lying on pine boughs and the definite beginnings of cramps twinging in my belly. But I'd never felt better. Sated. Happy—until I rolled to face the warm chest against my back.

Roan slept still, and heat radiated off him like a wood stove.

Fever…

My chest tightened as I pressed my hand against his forehead, and a hissed curse followed from my lips.

He's burning up.

Eyes stinging, I sat up, glancing around the immediate vicinity. Rock, lichen, brush, and blue sky. No humans. No vehicles, planes, or boats. No emergency room or pharmacy. How far to the Kelly homestead?

"Roan?"

He stirred at my voice, a groan rumbling his chest.

"Can you wake up? Look at me?"

He blinked, a grimace twitching his beard.

I cupped his cheek, patting a bit to help him wake. "Your

fever's back. We need to go before it gets too bad, okay? You need to get up." My voice rose with the beginnings of hysteria. I'd only just found my love, my life, and I refused to bear a broken heart again.

"Annie." Roan groaned and pushed up onto his elbow.

I grasped his shoulders and helped him sit up fully.

Head hanging low, shoulders rounded, he took a few deep breaths. "I'm good." A shiver wracked him against my hold. "Good," he repeated, his voice rasped and quiet.

Unable to reply past the thickness tightening my throat, I nodded and hopped up, shoved our blanket into the backpack, and tossed it around my shoulders. The straps hung way too long, so I quickly cinched them tight.

"You're bleeding."

I realized wetness seeped from me—my period.

"Fuck, Annie. I fuckin' hurt you."

"No." I muttered a curse, dropping the backpack to dig out my t-shirt soiled from smoke and soot. "It's just my period."

He sat quiet as I ripped strips from my shirt and shoved one into my panties without an ounce of embarrassment. We faced hunger and a debilitating disease in the wilderness. My monthly, womanly woes was the least of my concerns.

"I'll carry it." Roan's exhausted tone suggested he wouldn't hear an argument as I once more lifted the backpack, but I shot him a glare.

"It doesn't matter how we get there, who carries what, we just need to *go*," I bit out, my cramps intensifying as I stood.

He pushed up to stand, and I clasped his hand as he wavered unsteadily on his feet.

I couldn't bear to study his pale face, his glazed-over eyes. We didn't have much time.

"Stick to the river," he whispered. "Won't get lost."

"Okay." Squeezing his hand, I started off in my filthy socks, my mind preoccupied with worry to feel the soreness, the cuts and blisters from walking all but barefoot in the wilderness for two days.

We walked for hours, the sun beating down on us, Roan stumbling and slowing our progress. At least we moved.

Around lunchtime, I sat him by the river's edge and bathed his hot skin with one of the rinsed-out socks, helping to cool him just the slightest bit. I buried the bloodied rag I'd shoved in my panties, bulked up with two for the amount dripping from me, and we started out again while I popped olives into my mouth.

Roan had no appetite, nor did he later when we stopped for another break.

Within seconds of his sitting, he slumped to the side, eyes closed.

"Roan?" I slid off the pack and knelt, my hand going to his forehead.

He felt even warmer.

Tears slid down my cheeks.

"Roan?" I croaked his name.

"Rest."

"Okay." I sniffed and nodded, wiping the soiled sweatshirt sleeve over my face. "Okay. We'll rest. Let me know when you can go, okay? We have to keep moving."

He didn't rouse for hours, and I sat huddled beside him, focus on his face, my knees drawn up inside his sweatshirt as cramps continued to jab my belly like a knife. I'd wrapped the blanket around him, ticking it in tight, but he shivered so violently at times, the blanket dislodged.

Salty tear tracks stiffened the skin on my face. My nose continued to run.

I didn't light a fire—couldn't bear the thought of lighting a flame.

Once more, I buried the bloody period rags in case a predator sniffed their scent, their hunger like mine. By the time semi darkness took the summer night sky, I gave over to the truth we wouldn't be moving until morning.

Shivering, I crawled under the blanket to snuggle against Roan's heat. Closed my eyes. Held him close.

———

"Annie." Roan's whisper jerked my eyelids up to daylight, and I touched his burning face.

"I'm here."

He nuzzled my palm, a smile twitching his lips. "Sweet… My Annie."

"I am yours." Tears slipped down my cheeks, and I kissed his eyelids, his nose, his parted lips. He hadn't woken, merely muttered in delirium. "Always and forever if you'll have me."

"Mine."

I kissed him again. "Yes."

His hand found my hip, his grip hot. Firm. "Need."

"What do you need?" I whispered, moving where his hand guided, situating myself atop his laid-out form. The heat of his torso burned through my sweatshirt, but the hard ridge of his cock pressing against my core stirred warmth of a different sort.

"Roan," I whispered, wanting—but still bleeding.

He groaned, squeezing me tight, hips grinding against me. "Need," a mere whisper escaped his lips.

My stomach clenched at the thought we wouldn't make it, that the fever would take him from me before we reached his parents' homestead. I wanted him, needed him, too.

Throat once more choking me, I tried to shimmy out of his arms to rid of us the clothing keeping us apart. He wouldn't release me.

"Roan—let go for one second." I doubt he heard me in his fever-crazed state, but I continued to try to move. "I need too. Let me take off my panties and get rid of this messy rag. Let me free that python fighting to get to me, okay? Come on, big boy…let me move."

I managed to get my hand between us, slipped beneath the band of his sweats. A few more wiggles, and I freed his dripping length.

He wouldn't let up the banded arms around me, so I pulled the damp rag from my panties, flicked it away, and pushed the tatters of my panties to the side. A shift of my hips managed to get the thick head of his cock notched against my core wet with blood and arousal.

"Roan."

As though his body knew what the mind didn't, his hips lifted, and I clutched his waist tight with my thighs, pressing back to meet him.

"Oh, holy hell." I grit my teeth against the stretch. My body wasn't fully ready for him, and the second stinging pain rose from his steady forward movement, I pulled away, trying to better coat him with his pre-cum and blood.

He growled, tightening his arms on me, and pushed harder.

I gasped, tears streaming down my cheeks. Too much. Too thick.

Pain stung, cramped through me.

"Roan," I gasped his name, but still he pushed with steady force, and I told myself to relax so he wouldn't cause any damage.

He pulled out—thank fucking Christ—and thrust so damn

deep, so damn fast, he stole my breath, slammed into my cervix.

Too far down his torso, I couldn't kiss his lips as his body took over, rutting into me like a wild animal. With one hand trapped between our bodies, I only had one to touch his face. Smooth back his hair, try to erase the deep frown furrowing his brow as he took—and took.

The instinctive need driving him doused my pussy walls with arousal.

Muscles tight and hard locked around my body, squeezing the air from my lungs, and I cried, touching his face, his lips parted with grunts, telling him we would be okay. He would be okay. We *had* to—I couldn't imagine going on without him.

Other hand being where it lay trapped between us, I took advantage of that fact and slid my fingers around his thrusting length, the wetness from us both soaking him, soaking my panties shoved to the side.

I rubbed my slickened fingertips over my clit, thrumming as best I could, not even able to shift to fuck back onto him.

He'd taken my freedom to move, but I would have given up everything to feel what he did to me. Emotion ran my head amok, poured tears down my cheeks, off my chin, to drip onto his chest.

I held his cheek in one hand, my thumb on his lower lip, feeling the panted, hot breaths he expelled with every grunt and groan while thrusting steadily into me. Taking—and yet giving.

"Fill me up, Roan," I whispered, the words punched from my mouth with every sharp snap of his hips. "Give. Me. What. I. Need."

His abs and chest tightened beneath me, and he shoved me back to meet him.

So deep. "R-Roan!"

Wetness erupted deep inside me, and my pussy clamped around him, milking him, greedy for what he emptied into me. Heart racing, I clenched my eyes shut, cheek on his hot, hard chest, and rode the waves crashing over me, convulsing my body in his arms, the tingles racing clear to my toes and fingertips as his cock pulsed and pulsed. Filling me.

My heart ached as we stilled.

Our last time?

Tears soaked his t-shirt long before his arms went lax around me.

23

ROAN

So thirsty.

The words rang like a bell between my pounding temples. Pain throbbed through the rest of me, like I'd taken a tumble down a mountainside along with boulders and stone crashing against me.

A muffled groan reached through the pain, and I realized the rumble came from my own chest.

"Roan."

An angel's voice… My Annie.

Did I smile? I tried to.

A soft hand touched my cheek, my forehead, and I blinked at the sand in my eyes. Worked my tongue in the desert of my mouth.

"Here."

Coolness slid past my lips, and I swallowed by reflex, the cold water trickling clear to my stomach. "M-more," I rasped, and Annie held the back of my neck, lifting to better help me drink.

"It's the tin can," she said, pouring the most delicious coolness into my mouth. "Be careful with the sharp edge."

I remembered cutting at the can, creating something for us to drink from. I remembered walking in a fevered haze. I remembered the warm wetness of her pussy…from the night before? A week past?

"What d-day?" I managed as she set my head back down on the ground. Shivers slid over me, and she tucked the blanket around my shoulders.

"We only walked for two."

"T-two more t-to home," I managed through clattering teeth. Fuckin' wasted body. No way I would make it. "Y-you have t-to go, Annie."

"I'm not leaving you," she stated, the sharpness in her tone twitching my lips.

"G-got to. C-can't…"

She pressed her soft lips to mine, and I strained upward to keep them there when she lifted away.

"T-tease."

A soft snicker pried my eyelids up. I wanted to see her, see my Annie. My angel.

"Hi," she whispered, smoothing my hair off my forehead, her eyes dark, the purple hue beneath them enough to worry my guts into a knot.

"You need to g-go," I attempted to keep my tone firm and in control against the muscle spasms trying to keep my body warm. "Get Pa. B-bring him back."

"I can't make it without you," she choked.

"You're s-strong. I know you'll make it." I smiled, pain riddling me, but my heart swelling. "G-goshawk—you own the sky. So damn perfect. D-driven. You can d-do it." I clenched my teeth against the shivers wracking through me, and tears welled in her beautiful eyes, spilling down cheeks already lined by dirty tracks.

She nodded and sniffed, smoothing my forehead again.

I closed my eyes, dark exhaustion pulling on me. "Love you… Annie, girl…" The whisper died on my lips, but she let out a sob and teased me again with her mouth.

So damn soft.

So fuckin' *mine*.

I smiled, a sigh rushing through me.

Darkness took the pain away.

24

ANNIE

Hunger twisted my insides, and although I'd agreed to head off on my own, I refused to leave him vulnerable to the elements.

I built a pine bough lean-to over him. Filled the tin can to the brim, setting it close enough he could roll to reach it—but not knock it over if just thrashing around a bit. I also left his nearly empty pack and his knife alongside the cup. He wouldn't have allowed it had he been awake. Dad's bone-handled knife and the flint, I kept in the sweatshirt's front pocket.

Roan lay like the dead, unmoving except for an occasional shiver.

Hotter than the night before, I knew his fever bordered on the type that caused damage.

I shoved a six-foot stick into the ground in an open area just out of reach of the river, both of my ragged socks hanging limply at its top. A marker in the event Dad flew low enough to watch for us along the shore.

Teeth clenched to keep from more sobs, I finally turned away. The insides of my thighs stung, my core throbbed from how he'd fucked me the night before, but the reminder gave me something to focus on. Something to remember, to cling to as my body soaked the last rag I had left. When the time came, I would rip off the sleeve of a sweatshirt and create another pad.

Numbness crept over my feet during the cold night, and I stumbled forward, ever onward, alongside the river, always keeping it in sight. Moving among rock and around brush, every flutter of a bird, every scamper of a skittish critter kicking adrenaline through my system, giving me energy.

Hunger ate at my insides, clawing like a hissing cat. I doused her with cold water, taking the edge off every hour or so. At least I stayed hydrated.

My legs ached with fatigue, like leaden pipes, mere stumps of logs, moving on autopilot.

Ears straining for the sounds of Mom and Dad coming to search for us, I scanned the skies more than the unforgiving wilderness around me. Bright blue expanses, puffy, billowing white cotton balls dotted across its canvas. A screeching goshawk streaking by, the memory of Roan's words bringing a smile to my lips, but it disappeared on the horizon, fading from view, from my life.

I trudged uphill praying Roan wouldn't do the same. Stumbled downward.

Another step, and another stomachful of water.

A bear eyed me from the opposite shore, and I soaked in the adrenaline of fear even though I knew he couldn't reach me. I'd always feared running into a grizzly like Dad…

My feet hastened for perhaps a mile before the post-adrenaline crash came, leaching me of energy.

More damn tears rolled as the image of Roan's still body returned to haunt my mind. Would he live until I returned with his parents? Would a bear find him first? Rip into his flesh, lap at his warm, diseased blood? Would a pack of wolves tear him limb from limb, fighting over his hands, his entrails?

Sobs tore from my chest, and I clutched at the sweatshirt, stumbling forward.

Don't stop, Annie. Don't ever stop...

———

I woke, shivering in the rising sun.

Fever.

Jolting upright, I blinked myself fully awake, taking in the smoldering embers of the small fire I'd forced myself to build —and had dry-heaved over with fear. But I'd done it.

No fever, I realized as my mind woke. Just cold.

Hungry.

I stumbled the couple of yards from the ditch I'd curled up in the night before and drank long from the river rushing past beneath my face.

Cold and filling—my stomach cramped. I pushed up on my haunches, eyes closed, soaking in the sun's energy.

"Please..." I whispered, unsure who I prayed to. Mother Nature had thrust us together in the vilest way possible—I felt she ought to make things right.

Day four.

Perhaps I'd get lucky and reach the Kelly homestead before nightfall.

A snapping twig jerked my head around.

Golden eyes peered at me. Ragged gray fur covered its quivering body. Lips peeling back to emit a low growl.

Wolf.

Pulse crashing against my ears, I dropped my gaze to his massive paws, giving him my submission. My hand shook as

I inched it toward my waist, fumbling to find the sweatshirt's pocket opening.

He growled again—and I grasped Dad's bone-handled knife.

I shuddered like a damn leaf in a hailstorm, but Goddamnit, I'd had enough. Pulling the knife free, I lifted my gaze. Stared the scary as fuck beast right in the damn eyes. He eyed me like the piece of meat I was—bloody and probably fucking delicious smelling to his nose.

"Sick fuck," I hissed, pushing up to crouch, knife in front of me. "Want a taste of me you bastard?"

I waved the knife, my brain fuzzy, a sense of amusement wanting to bubble laughter inside me.

"Come and get it." I beckoned with my free hand, flashing him my own teeth as another growl rumbled his chest. "Come on."

He took a hesitant step my way, and I waved him forward.

"I'm a goddamn goshawk—I'll knife your eyes from your head!" I whispered harshly, adrenaline, fear, and sick exhaustion swirling in my stomach. All the water I'd drank rose up my throat, but I choked it down, my eyes stinging.

Two more steps brought him too close.

Too fucking close.

"Back the fuck up!" I hollered, waving my knife, my jagged fingernails digging into my palm.

He held my stare. Licked his chops.

I yanked the bloody rag from between my thighs and threw it at him. "Back the fuck up!" My shriek echoed as I stood fully.

He nosed my pad, gaze latched on me, and his nostrils flared, lips curling.

A snarl ripped loose from him, muscles bunched to

spring, and I shifted—as though in slow motion—settling my stance.

Knees slightly bent.

Dad's knife and my free handheld out in front of me.

The fucker leaped without a sound, my free arm blocking his snapping teeth by instinct—and his weight barreled into me, knocking me backward into the water.

I screamed against the pain from his gnawing teeth digging into my arm, his claws scrambling to tear my flesh. "Fucker! Fuck!" I stabbed through fur and bone. Stabbed again as water splashed over my face. I choked on the river, Dad's knife finding the wolf's side again and again as he ripped and tore at my arm still firmly clamped in his jaw.

"Die you piece of shit!" I sobbed, pushing against his weight to get leverage, get my head out of the water.

Golden eyes—fucking inches from my face—I screamed and thrust the blade into his ear.

He slumped off me with the same amount of sound as when he'd attacked.

Silent.

I heaved for breath, staring, water swirling around me.

Numb. No pain. No cold.

Pushing to my feet, I eyed the unmoving body of the wolf who thought he could defeat me, his life's blood swirling away from us in the river's current lapping at his still body.

Roan believed in me. Trusted me to save him.

I turned and stumbled away, blood dripping from the knife still clutched in my hand. Wet heat dripped from my core and down my arm beneath the tattered remains of the sweatshirt.

A burned-out grass tussock rolled my ankle as I made it up off the river's bank, and I dropped the knife. Sobbing, I pushed up, stumbled onward, too tired to search for the weapon.

Need to walk. Save Roan.

My stomach ached as much as my legs, my belly, and my arm, and I hunched over, watching through bleary eyes as I placed one foot in front of the other.

Another.

Another.

Too long—it's taking too long.

I'd been walking for days. Weeks. Had I somehow passed the homestead?

A buzz sounded in my ear, and I brushed at whatever damn bug wanted a taste of the sweat, blood, and the stench clinging to my skin. Damn thing grew louder. More insistent. Still, I waved my arms.

"Leave me alone!" I shrieked, sobs ripping from my chest as I attempted to cling to sanity. "Leave me alone!" Eyes clenched shut, hands dropping to fist at my sides, I screamed until my throat ached, my voice echoing in the distance.

The buzzing sounded louder as my voice faded away.

Plane...

I jerked my eyes open, a shot of delicious adrenaline pumping through my system with every heightened thump of my heart.

The engine roared closer, and I stumbled to turn around, realizing they approached from the south.

Metal—white and blue—glinted in the sunset, and I sobbed, somehow finding the energy to jump up and down, waving my arms.

Daddy. Please see me...

The day Annie had agreed to call us came and went, and worry settled in my gut, the kind that didn't allow me to sleep. We hadn't heard from her since the storm raged across the state's center. The call to her sat phone didn't go through. The old radio stayed silent.

I contacted Flynn Kelly an hour after both Jessie and I forced down some lunch and filled him in on Annie's call a few days earlier telling us about Roan's fever. Not wanting to worry his parents, Jessie and I had decided to not contact them until we got an update on how he fared.

Flynn said they'd been hit hard with rain and that the river had swelled considerably, but the mention of wildfire stilled my heart rate, brought my instinct to razor focus.

"The glow of the fire lay to the south, but the rain started long before it reached us."

I chewed over Flynn's words crackling over the radio. To the south—my homestead. "We can't reach Annie. She was supposed to call yesterday."

Flynn swore, as my sharpened brain formed a plan in under three seconds.

"Jessie and I will head toward the homestead. Stay put until you hear from us."

He argued, wanting to strike out across the burned land, but I begged him to stay put. We would reach the homestead long before he could—and cover fifty times the distance in searching if need be.

Within an hour, Jessie and I arrived at the hangar, supplies for any possibility in hastily packed bins. Pale and lips in a thin line, Jessie did a pre-fight check of her old Beaver while I did my own on the newer Cessna.

While anxiety continued to churn my damn guts, I tugged Jessie tight to my chest, my nose, and lips against her soft hair. "Let's go find our little girl."

She nodded against my chest, and I grasped her face when she pulled back. A lone tear slid down her cheek, and I brushed it away with my thumb, the worry in her blue eyes punching me in the gut. "It's going to be okay, Vixen."

"You don't know that," she whispered, more tears welling.

"We've got supplies for every emergency possible," I reminded her of our hustle to gather everything we thought we might need. "We'll be there in under forty minutes."

She blew out a heavy breath, and I quickly captured her lips, my blood stirring as it did every time I breathed her into my soul.

My Jessie—the breath in my lungs, the beat in my heart. But she'd started sharing those bits of me when our baby girl squawked for the first time. She'd gotten too big, too damn quick, and the thought of losing her…

Throat tight, I released my wife, and without another word, we climbed into separate cockpits. A few minutes later, I watched her take to the sky, banking as I sped after her down the river. The land fell away as I lifted, and I caught up to my wife, flying to her left. We'd laid out a plan after I'd gotten off the radio with Flynn—she would head north to the Kelly homestead and make her way southward in her search.

We soon split ways in the sky, and I headed toward our homestead alone, wanting to protect Jessie from what I feared to find.

Burned land.

Black and dead.

A shell of a cabin rather than the green and browns of life.

Throat tightening again, I buzzed low, circling our acreage twice. No evidence of life lay beneath me, but need like a goddamn tailwind thrusting me forward, had me angling toward the river again.

I had to know for myself. See with my own damn eyes— up close. I landed on the swollen waters and pulled up to the untouched wooden ramp.

"Annie!" I hollered the second I hopped from the plane.

No answer rose, so I quickly tied up and sprinted up the path, hollering my daughter's name on the way toward the burned-out cabin.

What was left of Annie's computer lay before the cabin's stoop. Bare footprints and a single boot print littered the soot around me.

They're alive.

My breath left in a rush, and I choked back a rising sob, fighting to keep hold of myself.

"Alive," I breathed the word out and took a deep breath, my nerves settling, and I once more homed in with deter- mined focus to find my little girl.

Making an ever-widening circle, I found where they'd taken to the hills that hadn't been touched by fire—but they'd come back down. Turning, I peered back toward the river— and quickly hurried that way after not finding evidence they'd gone cross-country through the burned land toward the Kelly's home.

I radioed Jessie to let her know I'd found signs of life and that the homestead would need to be rebuilt.

She'd flown over the Kelly's—but only their family of four had stood in their yard, waving.

"Let's find them," she whispered, her voice broken.

"I'll head upriver."

Jessie said she'd head inland, fly as the crow would between homesteads, even though I hadn't found any evidence they'd taken the more direct route.

A few minutes later, I flew low along the river's edge, to my left, blackened earth and stubs of trees, to my right, the land teamed with life, green and thriving beneath the summer's late afternoon sun. Even though I didn't think the two kids would have been able to get to the shore's better side, I studied both, my eyes straining, flitting side to side.

The Kelly homestead didn't lay a mile northward from my location when I caught sight of a flash of red along the black shore. With every yard flying past beneath me, the form took shape—definitely human. Red sweatshirt. Pale legs and long, dark hair.

She turned, arms waving, and recognition lit my insides like a fucking burst of fireworks.

"Baby girl," I choked out the words and buzzed past her, our gazes connecting. "Jessie," I called through the radio, "I found her."

26

ANNIE

Dad…my precious, fucking *fabulous* dad, buzzed low along the river, his gaze latching onto mine as he flew past.

"Daddy," I whimpered as he banked. Still waving, laughing, and crying, damn near mad, I called out to him a dozen more times while he circled around and flew past again.

Rocks and boulders littered the river where I travelled, and I knew he'd have to fly away from sight in order to land.

He'd found me.

I hurried northward, my hopes flying higher than any plane, than any hawk in the sky.

Hopefully, a deep enough section of river lay not too far away, enough he could put down on the water and make his way on foot to me.

Rescue had come. I just hoped we'd get back to Roan before it was too late.

Still stumbling, I pressed onward, waiting for the plane's engine or his calls, my body numb to pain from adrenaline.

Dad's voice reached me first, and the tears started up again.

"Here!" I cried out, half-laughing, half-crying.

He rounded a boulder a few hundred yards upriver. Tall and strong. Fully bearded, broad shoulders stretched by a black flannel, a huge pack strapped on his back.

Daddy.

Tears streamed down my cheeks, and my knees gave way, sinking me to the pebbled shore I'd followed for what seemed weeks.

"Annie!" he hollered, relief in his voice, and sprinted my way.

Tears filled his eyes as he dropped to the ground and pulled me in tight to his chest.

Safe. Rescued.

I clung to him.

"You okay, baby girl?"

"Roan," I forced out through my sobs. "Fever—south."

"We're going to get him. Everything is going to be okay, now. I got you."

Dad rocked me a bit until I quieted, and I pushed back, wiping my face on the sleeve of the sweatshirt.

"You're covered in blood," Dad rasped, pulling at the sweatshirt, his hands frantic. "You're bleeding—fuck, Annie…"

"Wolf got my arm—but I stuck him in the ear with your knife."

Dad stilled, his dark eyes flitting over my face.

"Got my damn period, too, not that you want to know about that," I muttered.

He swore and pulled me against his chest again.

"I'm getting blood all over your nice flannel."

"Don't give a shit. Sure you're okay?" He pulled away, once more checking me over. "Take this goddamn thing off," he said, pulling up on the sweatshirt.

Pain rippled up my arm, but I bit my tongue to keep from crying as we finagled the soaked, ragged thing over my head. I sat naked and shivering as Dad eyed my arm and yanked the backpack off him.

He called Mom to let her know I was okay while pulling out everything I could need from his backpack: clean clothes, socks and boots, food, and a thick blanket. Uncaring of my state or undress, I stripped off my ruined panties and pulled on the clean, warm clothes over my torso before washing up enough in the river for new panties, and an extra sock to act as a pad.

Dad studied me while I sat on a rock and wiggled into a pair of warm sweatpants. "My strong, baby girl. How did you survive the fire?"

"Roan took me into the river. Held me tight to keep me from being swept away in the current."

His gaze softened as he crouched down and smoothed back my tangled hair. "You love him."

"Always have," I whispered, my smile wobbling.

"He's a good man—you couldn't do better."

"So, you approve?"

"Always have," Dad echoed, his dark eyes series. "How far south is he?"

"I-I really don't know. I left him this morning and it feels like I walked for days. I left my socks hanging like a flag closer to the river down the bank from where he is."

"Must have missed it." Dad pulled out his phone and called Mom again, telling her what to watch for.

She flew past a few minutes later, waving out the window. She headed southward to search the shore for my flag and hopefully find Flynn.

I picked up the boot Dad had left for me, sniffing back

tears that had poured the second I'd caught sight of Mom. "Not sure I can wear these boots, Dad."

He turned from digging a protein bar and bottle of water from his pack. "Shit." Lips in a thin line, he held my foot and studied what I couldn't bear to look at. "You're cut up pretty bad, but there's no sign of infection."

He'd brought along a first aid kit and took a bit of time to clean up my feet with water from the river first, before dousing both with hydrogen peroxide.

Bandages wrapped clear to my ankles, and he gently pulled up socks to cover them.

But the boots wouldn't fit.

Dad's phone rang. "It's Mom—yeah, vixen?" He peered at me with the same dark eyes I'd inherited while Mom spoke. He gave me a thumbs up, mouthing that she'd found Flynn.

"Is he okay?" I whispered, hinging on hope.

He gave me another thumbs up—so alive, at least.

A rushed exhale left me, and I worried my lower lip with my teeth while waiting for him to get off the phone.

"Okay," he finally told her. "Stay put. We'll come to you."

"What?" I asked the second he lowered the phone from his ear.

"He's got a wicked high fever, but he roused a bit for your mom. She got some liquid Tylenol into him and gave him a shot of antibiotics."

"Thank God," I whispered, my eyes welling again.

Dad eyed my bandaged feet while putting the sat phone in his pant pocket. "Think you can handle the backpack if I carry you piggyback out of here?"

"Can you handle us both?" I teased through my tears, not doubting my daddy's strength.

"The Cessna is less than a mile upriver. Cakewalk, baby girl."

27

ANNIE

What had seemed like hundreds of miles I'd travelled that morning ended up being closer to five. It took Dad mere minutes to spot Mom's plane tied to the riverbank, and in twice as many minutes, he landed and hopped out to toss the rope to Mom who waited on shore.

Even though she laughed and waved at me, tears rolled down her cheeks.

Dad carried me to her, gingerly set me on my feet, and Mom hugged me tight.

"How is he?" I asked the same time Mom asked the same about me. "I'll be fine," I answered first.

"The Tylenol hasn't kicked in yet. He's burning up—we have to get him into Fairbanks, Brock."

Dad lifted and spun me around onto his back like I weighed nothing more than a bag of groceries.

Mom led the way.

"She's got one fine ass," Dad said about Mom, and I punched his arm even though I knew he tried to lighten my worry.

"She's the best," I said instead, so overwhelmed with

emotion, I wanted to sleep for a week straight—once Roan was properly taken care of and on the mend.

My throat tightened to find he laid exactly as I'd left him that morning. Laid out and unmoving, our filthy blanket replaced with a clean one Mom must have brought.

Dad set me down at his side, and I smoothed back his hair, drinking in the sight of his pale face, his parted lips, hating that shivers still shook his poor body.

"Roan?" I whispered as Mom and Dad spoke quietly behind me. He didn't respond, so I leaned down and kissed his warm lips. "You're going to be okay," I whispered against his mouth. "Promise."

"We're going to get him out of here," Dad said, squatting down beside me. "I'm going to take you back to the hangar, and Mom will head north to pick up Flynn. She'll meet us there."

Sniffing, I nodded.

"You need to get checked out, too."

"Okay."

Dad took me to the plane first, and the two of us laid down the seats to open up the cargo area. I made up a quick blanket bed for Roan, and it took all three of us—Dad, Mom, and me to get him laid out in the back.

He groaned a few times, and I curled up against his side, shushing him, telling him everything was going to be okay. Within minutes of being settled, the shivers twitching him against me stopped. The Tylenol must have gotten into his system.

Neither Mom nor Dad spoke a word about me buckling into a seat, and a short time later, my belly dipped as Dad took us up into the sky.

The noise of the aircraft deafened, but I continued to murmur against Roan's ear, my fingertips smoothing over his hot forehead, his beard, his lips. A few tears fell, but ones of happiness and from having a sense of hope.

While a small clinic lay an hour south of home, I expected Dad would drive Roan straight into Fairbanks like Mom suggested. My second cousin something or other removed worked at the hospital, staying in Alaska when her parents had moved to California years earlier. Kari didn't share a name or physical characteristics with Mom. Leggy, tall, and brunette, she took after her father's side of the family.

She was also smart as shit and had gotten her master's in nursing. I'd stayed with her when Roan had come into town and knowing family would be on hand to care for my Roan set me at ease.

Roan's lips moved beneath my fingertips, and I pushed up onto my elbow to lean over him. He blinked, his eyes still glazed.

"Hey," I said even though I didn't think he wouldn't hear me over the noise of the plane's engine. I kissed him again, and his lips twitched beneath mine. "We're taking you to the hospital. You're going to be okay," I murmured into his ear, and a heavy sigh warmed my fingertips I left on his lips. "They'll have you fixed up in no time."

Roan shifted, his hand fumbling against my belly. I moved the blanket from atop him and grasped his hand, smiling when his fingers closed around mine in a gentle squeeze.

He rested, and we landed a few minutes later.

With the help of the mechanic Dad had radioed in to meet us at the hangar, they moved Roan into Dad's SUV, curled on his side on the back seat, his head resting on my lap. I played with his too-long hair, tucking the filthy strands away from his forehead and ear. A shuddering sigh left him—and I caught the sound of an incoming plane.

"Mom's almost here," I told Roan, searching the sky through the windows while Dad finished putting his plane away. "She went to get your dad."

"Pa…hates town," Roan muttered his first words, and sudden lightness bubbled up inside me.

"There they are," I told him, watching as Mom's old Beaver came into sight. "A couple of hours, and you'll be in good hands."

Roan didn't respond, and I let him sleep.

28

___

ANNIE

Mom had left her sat phone with Saige for them to keep better in touch. She also insisted I go to the emergency room, too, to get my feet checked out even though I didn't want to leave Roan's side.

We ended up in ER beds beside one another, the curtain pulled back so I could keep an eye on him as two nurses cut his filthy clothes off his body. Shivering and pale, his form still looked magnificent, and I clenched my jaw over the fact two other women got to see *my* man in all his naked glory.

Kari wasn't on duty, so another doctor took charge, checking over Roan, ordering an IV and meds, and then taking care of my feet and arm.

My feet didn't need stitches, but I ended up with a prescription for antibiotics to keep any brewing infection from taking over. I also got the first of four rabies vaccines just in case that fucking wolf slobbered shit into the gashes stitched shut on my arms.

Kari rounded the curtain as the nurse finished going over my discharge papers, her gaze flitting from Roan straight to me. "Jessie said you guys had quite an adventure."

156

I snorted a sarcastic laugh. Mom, Dad, and Flynn had gone for coffee a few minutes earlier after I insisted I was fine and wanted to be alone with Roan—not that I'd gotten more than two seconds before Kari had arrived. "Adventure —you could say that."

"Your dad said there isn't anything left of the homestead." Kari went straight to Roan, checking over his chart, eyeing his IV.

"It was horrible." A shiver slid through me at the memory of the fire.

"Are you okay, Annie?" Concern laced Kari's tone even though she didn't look away from my man.

"I will be," I whispered, knowing I'd dealt with and beat PTSD once before. "It'll just take time."

Kari checked Roan's temperature then turned toward me.

"Will he be okay?" I asked, my focus on Roan's still form.

"He'll be fine."

I slumped back from my seated position, a heavy exhale sinking me onto the hard hospital bed.

"Did you get your books written?" Kari asked, and the image of the melted MacBook surfaced in my memory.

"Yeah—but I lost everything in the fire."

"Shit."

I squeezed my eyes shut to keep the tears from flowing. "Yeah."

Kari squeezed my good hand. "You need to go home and rest."

"I'm not leaving him." My eyelids popped open.

My whatever-removed cousin smiled down at me, her golden-brown eyes full of emotion I couldn't quite name while flitting over my bandaged arm and feet. "You need to go home," she repeated, her tone firm. "Rest. He's not going anywhere for a few days."

I swallowed and nodded my agreement.

"You love him?"

I didn't hesitate to nod again.

Another smile flitted over Kari's lips, but it appeared forced, that emotion swelling in her eyes again. "I hope he's everything you've dreamed of Annie. I hope he looks at you like you make the sun rise and the stars shine."

"He does," I whispered, my throat still tight.

"Don't let him get away," Kari whispered back and squeezed my hand again. "Call me if you need anything, okay?"

I watched her leave, but my wandering mind shut off whatever Kari struggled with as Mom and Dad returned, Roan's Pa on their heels.

Dad pushed a wheelchair—for me, I realized, knowing I wouldn't be walking out of the hospital. He lifted and settled me in the chair and wheeled me to Roan's side so I could say goodbye.

I held his hand, caressing up to his elbow to find his temperature had cooled considerably.

Flynn eyed me from across his son's torso. "He's going to be fine," his deep voice rumbled, and I nodded. "I'll watch over him for you."

Tears once more hazed my vision, and I choked out my thanks, happy to know Roan wouldn't be alone.

"I'll be back in the morning," I whispered to Roan and kissed his fingertips one at a time.

Dad turned the wheelchair, and we left Flynn and Roan behind in the middle of a city—in the middle of the night.

Laying down on the backseat of Dad's SUV, I fell asleep

within minutes, barely rousing when he carried me into our house hours later and laid me in my bed.

Mom whispered something about a shower to me, but I shook my head and buried my face in my pillow, the scent of dryer sheets and home settling my muscles and bones.

I passed the hell out—and stayed out in a dreamless sleep of pure exhaustion. No yellow flames, no golden wolf eyes.

Just pure, necessary rest.

29

ROAN

Sharp scents assaulted me, and I wrinkled my nose, turning my face, hoping to escape them.

A rough palm pressed against my forehead, and I peeled an eyelid open to find Pa alongside me in a bath of sunlight.

Bright.

I closed my eyes again and tried to find my bearings.

"We're in Fairbanks," Pa said, and I forced my eyes open again, struggling to get a grip on where I was, why my brain fuzzed like a newborn chicken.

Beeps and murmured voices echoed in my ears, pulling my brow into a deep frown. "L-loud."

He chuckled and sat back in the chair alongside me. "*Too* loud," he agreed.

Fairbanks.

Annie.

I turned my head, the smooth walls and nose-stinging smells still hitting my nose letting me know where I was.

"Where's Annie?"

"She's at home."

"She's okay," I released the words on a rushed exhale of breath I hadn't realized I'd held.

"She's fine. Feet and arm are pretty ripped up, but she'll heal up fine."

I closed my eyes and sank back onto the pillow, taking stock of my body. The pain I'd last remembered feeling when telling Annie to leave me behind had lessened considerably, but I still felt like absolute shit.

"Am I going to be okay?" I muttered, feeling weak as a newborn.

"Doctor came in about an hour ago. Said you'll be out of here within a day or two."

"Thank fuck."

Pa chuckled again. "Can't say I'm fond of being in the city, either."

"How's the homestead? Ma and the twins?" I asked as soon as the wildfire memory trickled back into my brain.

"Homestead escaped the fire, and all my girls are right as the rain that saved us."

My lips twitched, but flatlined at the memory I had nothing of my own, nothing to offer the woman I'd told I loved.

She'd lost everything in that fire, all her hard work, but I didn't doubt her ability, her drive to rewrite and finish what she'd set out to do, same as she'd saved me.

But she would chase that dream again from her parents' house, far from my world.

No more Charran homestead meant no more Annie in close proximity.

My chest ached like a knife dug in deep, twisting, tearing into flesh, and I swore my life's blood drained from my pumping heart.

Pa kept quiet, and I eventually slipped back into darkness, the numb kind that eased both physical and emotional pain.

———

A soft hand on my brow roused me again, and I turned my face to nuzzle against the scarred palm.

My sweet Annie.

Warmth rolled through me, but reality slammed into me like a gale wind sweeping straight off a snow-capped mountain. I would return to the wilderness. She would stay in town to chase her dreams.

"How are you?" she whispered, her hand going to my forehead again.

"Better, but really weak. Stink like a damn animal. Need a fuckin' shower," I muttered, making her smile.

"You are pretty stinky."

"While I'm looking forward to a *real* shower, I can't wait to get out of here," I told her, glancing around the sterile room. "Can't stand the smell of the chemicals, and the noise?" I grimaced, turning back toward Annie. "Can't wait to get home."

She wiped her forearm across her eyes and nodded, looking down at our clasped hands rather than my face.

My Annie—my love. The one woman I wanted, one I couldn't provide for.

Shoulders slumped, she sat in silence, and I couldn't find the fuckin' words to make her smile. Couldn't figure out a way to make her mine—and keep her happy.

"How are your feet?" I croaked, needing to fill the strange silence between us.

"Better. I hobbled in on my own."

I nodded, unsure what else to say. While my heart ached

to beg her to come back with me, shack up in my parents' cabin with me, I wanted more for her.

Loving Annie at that point in our lives meant letting her go.

"My arm hurts more."

I flicked my focus down to the arm resting in her lap—bandaged from elbow to wrist. "The hell?"

"A wolf attacked me."

I stared at Annie's unblinking eyes. "What?"

"A hungry wolf who somehow survived the fire like us. He thought he could eat me for dinner, but I introduced him to Mr. Bone-Handled Knife."

I snorted a chuckle. "The fuck you say."

"Right in his ear," she whispered without smiling, recreating the stabbing motion with her bandaged arm.

Holy fuckin' hell, my woman was more than a hawk in the sky.

Not mine.

"Promise me you'll finish that book, Annie," I croaked past the thickening in my throat.

The unhappiness in her eyes, the overwhelming emotion in them made me close mine. Couldn't fuckin' handle not being enough for her. Fuckin' failure in life.

"I promise," she whispered.

I swallowed, squeezed her hand, and nodded, a cold block of ice settling into my gut. Shivers didn't twitch over me, but the ice sliding through my veins hurt worse than any fever.

When she and her Mom left a few hours later, I told Pa I needed to get the hell out of there. Needed to get away from the stink and noise, needed to get away from Annie since being near her and knowing I couldn't have her hurt worse than any fuckin' disease.

Brock flew us back to the homestead the next day.

Annie hadn't come to see me off. Hadn't begged me to stay—but I would have had she'd asked, no matter how much I hated being around so many people. I would have moved fuckin' mountains, grit my teeth against the constrictive sense civilization held over me, anything to make her happy.

She let me go, so I did the same, hoping my little goshawk would own the skies and find someone worthy of her, someone who could support her in ways I couldn't.

30

ANNIE

I laid in my bed, the soft feather pillow beneath my head catching my tears.

Roan had left. He'd hated every second of his hospital stay that I'd seen. Hated the noise, the smell of cleaning products, the constant bustle of people coming and going.

He belonged to the wilderness.

I would have gone back with him if he'd asked. I would have left everything behind, lived in a tent, hell, a damn cave, if it meant being with him. I would have agreed to damn near anything to stay at his side.

Dad had flown him and his pa back to the homestead without wasting a minute stopping by our house to say goodbye, and I hated all three of them for the emptiness in my heart.

Our time had ended—once again because of a fire.

Roan had chased down my heart, had taken my body, my love—but too much stacked against us.

I rolled, eyeing my ancient desk top computer. While all my old notes and a few hastily typed scenes lay on the hard drive, everything I'd written over the previous weeks had melted away into nothing.

Start from scratch or scratch the idea of writing entirely from my mind? The overwhelming knowledge of what I would have to rewrite, all I'd lost, tempted me to move on, do something else with my life like my ex had always pushed me to do.

A quiet knock sounded.

"Yeah?" I called, rolling onto my back again.

Mom stuck her head in my doorway, a frown on her face. "Justin is here and asking to see you."

My frown dented my forehead, same as hers. "What does he want?" I spit out the words, hating that the heartache my ex had caused earlier in the spring slammed into me, ripping me to shreds again even though I held not one ounce of love in my heart for him.

"He said he wanted to make sure you're okay."

I snorted and pushed up to sit against my headboard. "Like he really cares," I muttered grabbing my pillow and holding it against my stomach. "Send the asshole in."

Mom smirked. "Justin!" she hollered. "Come on up!" A wink, and she whispered, "Give him hell."

"Don't worry," I whispered right back, narrowing my gaze. He'd hurt me, left me near speechless when breaking up with me, but I'd found a part of myself in the wilderness. Strength and resilience I'd set aside in submission to him. I wasn't the Annie he'd known back in April.

And I sure as hell wasn't going to give up on my dreams.

"Hey." Justin's blond head poked through my door, same as Mom's had, his blue eyes full of concern.

I held in my snort, simply raised an eyebrow in question, the lack of longing stirring inside me for his touch twitching my lips.

He cleared his throat and moved into the room, shoving his hands into his jeans' pockets. "I just wanted to make sure you're okay."

"And why would you care?"

"I *do* care, Annie."

"Could have fooled me," I muttered, holding his stare.

His brow furrowed and smoothed out quickly. "Don't be like that."

"Like what? A woman who had her eyes opened to the true assholishness of her ex-boyfriend?"

"Annie—"

"How did you even find out I'd been hurt?"

"News travels fast in tiny towns. I gotta be truthful…" Justin moved into my room and sat on the edge of my bed without being invited, "…when I heard, I couldn't breathe."

"Funny, that's the same way I felt when you broke up with me after what seemed like four pretty damn good years together."

"I'm sorry." His blue eyes begged forgiveness, same as his tenor voice inflected with all sorts of pain and remorse that came much too late.

"Well, I'm not."

That groove appeared in his forehead again. "You can't mean that."

I let out a sigh. "I'm not sorry you broke up with me, Justin. It was for the best. Sure, you hurt me, and your lack of faith in me and my dreams hurts if I think on it, but any lovey dovey feelings I had for you are long gone."

He swallowed. "Y-you can't mean that. All those years of hard work you're willing to just toss away?"

"*You* did the tossing," I reminded him, "and I *do* mean it. I'm not the pushover, submissive woman who tripped over her own feet to please you, Justin. That woman is gone. And hard work?" I snorted. "Please. You had it easy."

"You said I was your world, Annie. Your man. What changed?"

"What changed," I said, hating that my throat tightened, "is that I found myself. My *own* world. I can stand on my own two feet, and I don't need a man to make me happy."

Roan made me so much happier, though.

Throat tight, I tossed aside the pillow I clutched to my center and scooted to the opposite side of the bed. "If you don't mind, I've got work to do."

"Still following that silly dream?" he asked as I sat in front of my computer.

"Always," I shot over my shoulder, my tone hard. "It's my passion in life—something you never supported."

"Annie, you've got to think realistically."

I *hated* that fucking tone he took with me, talking down to me as though he knew better than what fate might have in store for me.

"The chances are stacked up against you," he continued. "You're better off teaching creative writing or eighth-grade Language Arts like you went to college for."

"Again, you prove your worthlessness in my life."

"Annie!"

"Get out, Justin." I turned toward my slow as hell booting computer. "You've made it quite clear your selfish ass can't put a woman first in his life—and I won't settle for anything less."

Roan had put me first—my life—even over my writing, the thing I held dearest. The continued beat of my heart had meant more to him than anything, and I'd never told him how much I loved him. Needed him.

"I can change," Justin tried to persuade, and I brushed off his hand he placed on my shoulder while scooting my chair in closer.

"I don't care."

"Come on, Annie. Give me another chance."

"Again with the commands rather than asking or begging like a man truly in love would do," I muttered. "Get out, and don't ever come back, Justin. I have zero time for a man like you in my life."

I clicked on the mouse trying to hurry things along, tension riding my entire body.

His presence hovered. "Annie—"

"You lost your chance. Out."

Before I stab you *in the ear with a damn knife!*

The door clicked quietly shut a few seconds later, and I let out a heavy exhale, relaxing back into my chair and closing my eyes. While I expected more emotion, some sort of ache in my heart, all that coursed through me was relief at having him gone.

But the best thing about his visit? I vocalized what I needed to hear again. I'd found my own world. I'd found my strength—without a man.

A burning ember of desire of a different sort stirred inside my chest. Bitch Annie, even bitchier muse, rose to life, pushing aside the depression that had hung over me since Dad had taken Roan back home.

I have a story to tell, my characters reminded me. Their story needed to get into the hands of the readers who needed their happily-ever-after—even if I could never have one of my own in the way I wanted.

Driving need sat me up, and I clicked open a blank document.

Time to get to work.

Lips in a firm line, I placed my hands on the keyboard and started from the beginning—again.

31

ROAN

"You're a miserable bastard," Nissa muttered under her breath and cast out into the river.

I ignored her, same as I'd done since returning home a few weeks earlier. Didn't have much to say. Didn't know how to deal with the constant ache in my chest.

Ciarra, Ma, and Pa knew better than to try to dig into my head, but Nissa…

"And you're a pain in my ass," I tossed back, reeling in my lure.

"Maybe you love her because she's the only girl you've ever met. You're big, strong, and handsome—a perfect book boyfriend," she continued on talking at me like she knew better. "Go to town again. You could have your choice of women."

"I'm the only man outside Pa, Brock, and Junior you've ever met," I tossed back.

"I've met dozens between the pages of good books. Too many to choose from, actually," Nissa argued. "I think a woman should be able to have more than one."

"The hell you talking about, Nis?"

"I read this one book where two guys and a girl—"

"Yeah," I cut her off with a grimace. "I started that one and didn't finish. The thought of sharing Annie with anyone, male or female, raises my hackles."

Nissa let out an exaggerated sigh. "Why don't you radio her and just ask her to come live with us."

I glanced over at my young sister, reminding myself she knew nothing about the ways of the world—of men, relationships, or sex. Ma and Pa might be able to keep quiet when in their bed, but no way in hell my Annie could when my hands were on her.

My dick swelled to life, and I muttered a curse, teeth clenched as I cast again. Damn fish weren't biting. Damn balls ached, too. At least I'd kicked tularemia's ass and made a full recovery—with the help of a heavy dose of antibiotics, rest, and Ma's care.

I'd rather it had been Annie's.

I wanted her at the homestead. In *my* bed. Under my body, wiggling and whimpering, her wet heat tight around me even as she clung with her hands as though I was her rock, her foundation.

If only I were enough...*had* enough. While I had a lump sum in my bank account back in town, I'd be old and gray before I could afford to pay for a plot of land and build her a cabin. Black depression rose from where I'd attempted to tamp it down, choking out all life in my dick.

"I know if a man loved me like you do Annie, I'd move heaven and hell to be with him," Nissa continued quietly. "I'd live in a lean-to out here in the wilderness."

"And freeze to death come October," I attempted to burst her bubble with the cold facts of Alaskan living.

"A cave," she continued as though I hadn't spoken a bit

harsher than I'd intended. "We'd burrow into a nice den like bears and snuggle until springtime."

I barked a laugh—couldn't help myself even though heaviness sat on my chest like a damn boulder. "It's time Ma and Pa sent you off to the real world."

"Right?" She smiled brightly, her eyes shining at me. "I keep begging, but they say I'm too young. I'm eighteen!"

Still a baby.

My smile faded as I cast one last time. She had no fuckin' clue about life, having lived sheltered all her years. Ma and Pa had kept themselves secluded in the wilderness, probably to the point of being unhealthy, but I couldn't find fault. They lived for each other, always hanging on one another. Touching in some way. While their love didn't appear fragile in any way, it's almost like they feared facing reality.

Reality.

Something I'd seen more of first-hand than I ever wanted too again.

But I wouldn't fault Ma and Pa for raising us in the way they had, either. The wilderness was my home, same as they'd made it theirs.

I glanced over the mountains across the river, drinking in the wide-open expanse of nothing but Mother Nature and peaceful quiet.

"Jessie offered to get you a job once, right?" Nissa broke that peace.

"Yeah, but I'm a man, so don't get any ideas."

"Meaning a woman can't do the same things a man can?" she shot back, her snippy tone reminding me of Annie.

"That's not what I'm saying," I grumbled, rubbing at my chest, hating that damn near *everything* reminded me of the dark-haired woman of my dreams. "I just mean that you're still an innocent kid. You have no fuckin' clue what's out there. The type of people who would take advantage of you. Men who would try to take—steal from you."

"I'd hoof 'em in the danglies if they tried."

I barked another laugh, knowing she would—fuck knew I'd gotten her foot to my groin a few times. "Maybe next summer I'll take you and Ciarra to town for a weekend or something."

"Really?" She breathed the word, her eyes popping wide.

The idea of being around all that noise and bustle tightened my guts, but if it meant getting to see Annie again… "Yeah. Really."

"Is Pa expecting a delivery?"

"Not that I know of, why?"

Nissa nodded her head to the east. "Plane."

I jerked my head up faster than a grizzly can snap its jaws. The buzz reached my ears as the black dot in the distance grew into something recognizable, something the unmistakable noise of the engine had already revealed.

"Come on," I gathered up my fishing supplies and hurried up to the cabin. "Pa!"

He stepped out onto the stoop, wiping his hands on a towel, his gaze going straight to the incoming plane.

"You call for a delivery?" I asked, hurrying toward him.

"No." Brow furrowed, he kept his focus on the sky over my shoulder.

I quickly put my stuff away and came back outside to find Ma joining us from where she'd been picking berries up the hill.

She took Pa's hand, the other grasping at his elbow. "Flynn?"

Pa kept quiet, but his brow smoothed out as the plane drew closer, its blue and white logo revealing who it belonged to. He started toward the river, Ma clinging to him like always. I followed on their heels, straining my eyes for a glimpse of the occupants.

Brock did a fly by, while my sisters giggled and waved, and my heart fell at seeing him alone. He banked and landed on the water, the engine soon dying out to bring back the quiet.

If only my heart rested as peacefully as the silence beyond our feet on the pebbled path.

Brock hopped from the cockpit, tossed Pa a rope, and I stood on shore, feet planted solidly, catching his gaze.

He dipped his head in greeting, but clasped Pa's hand first.

"Everything okay?" Pa asked, and Brock nodded, his focus once more flitting my way.

"Yep. Just wanted to have a word with your son."

He'd flown all the way out here…to talk to me. My heart took to galloping, and I opened my mouth to ask if Annie was okay, but I reminded myself he'd said everything *was*.

After handing off a box of snickers to Nissa and Ciarra, and a few boxes of staples to Ma and Pa, Brock stood before me. The two of us close to the same height—same shoulder width—but gray shot through the dark hair by his temples and through his full beard while mine remained untouched by age.

"How is she?" I asked, my tone unsteady as hell.

"Healthy," Brock said, his dark eyes so damn familiar, I rubbed at my chest.

I could hear the suggestion of more in his tone and pressed for more. "But?"

"How are *you*?" Brock asked rather than answer.

"Life's fuckin' miserable," I muttered, glancing once more out over Mother Nature, wishing she could wipe out the shit inside my head and heart.

"Annie needs a hell of a lot more life than the one she's living right now, too."

I hated the thought she might be as miserable as me. "Is she writing?"

"It's all she does."

I nodded, happy to hear at least she still chased her dreams.

"Do you love her, Roan?" Brock's quiet question jerked my focus his way, and I held his piercing stare.

"Yes," I didn't hesitate to answer. "With every fuckin' bone in my body. I'd give my last breath for her. Face another damn wildfire bare-assed naked if it meant having her again."

His beard twitched like he held back a grin. "I was hoping you'd say that."

I tipped my head to the side, studying his growing smile. "What's on your mind, sir?"

Brock clasped my shoulder. "I think I know the perfect way to end both your misery and help her heal."

"I'm not moving into town," I shot out, going against the fact I'd all but told him I'd do anything for her, and when it came right down to it, I definitely would—if that's what she asked of me.

"Wouldn't ever suggest it," Brock said with a chuckle. "See, I've got a problem, too, and I think you're the man for the job."

32

———

ANNIE

I drank too much coffee, too much wine. Ate too many olives.

I also gained ten pounds and gave myself carpel tunnel in the days running together of nothing but writing—but I finished.

The fucking end.

Sitting back, I took a deep breath and let it slowly eek from my parted lips. Done. I'd written three novels in two months. My trilogy sat completed, my characters finally got their happily ever after—and I'd had two agents chomping at the bit and emailing me every other day for the final manuscript.

Both had made offers of representation, but I waited for feedback from the final book before deciding.

I glanced outside, rolling my shoulders, and blinking at finding snow flying.

Shit. How long have I been holed up in here?

Rubbing at my stiff neck, I pushed up from my chair. A few quick stretches to loosen muscles too-long lax, and I

177

went to peer out the window. An early snow, something I used to love as a kid, coated the ground.

The thought of the long winter ahead since I'd finished writing tore away my initial happiness over the cover of white…I had nothing to do.

Write another book.

I scowled at my muse's suggestion. "I need a fucking break, my damn wrist aches, and let's not jump the gun. I haven't landed a contract yet."

"Annie!" Mom hollered, and I pulled open my door.

"Yeah?" I called down the stairwell.

"You coming down for dinner tonight?"

"Yeah!"

"Yeah?" Her heightened tone suggested surprise—but the way I'd been over the months, ignoring the call to come down for meals, she should have been.

"I finished!" I hollered back.

Mom appeared at the foot of the stairs, oven mitts on her hands, her smile wide. "You finished."

I nodded and grinned, the sense of accomplishment making me want to jump up and down, wiggle around like a toddler dancing to a good beat.

"I'm proud of you, baby girl."

"Thanks."

Mom glanced down over me and snickered. "Why don't you get a shower, put on something more than pj's and join me tonight for a girls-only dinner celebration."

"Where's Dad?"

"Still away on business—but he should be back in a day or two. I'll open a bottle of wine and we can toast to your accomplishment. Girls' night and chocolate for dessert."

I hopped in the shower, ready to do as Mom suggested.

Two weeks later, I sat at dinner with both her and Dad, and I had news that had my heart thrumming.

"My agent got me a contract with one of the biggies in New York."

Dad stopped eating to look at me, but Mom's squeal and jumping up to hug me pulled my attention off his unmoved face.

"I'm so proud of you! So excited!" Mom hugged and bounced a bit, pulling a laugh from me, same as she'd done days earlier when we'd shared two bottles of wine and got a little drunk.

Dad cleared his throat and stood up, opening his arms wide. "You grew up too damn fast, baby girl, but I'm so proud of you."

I stepped into his hug, and he squeezed me tight.

"This mean you're leaving us for the east coast?" he asked, his tone guarded.

Pulling back, I frowned up at him. "No way in hell."

"You aren't signing with them?"

I smirked up at my old man. "Electronic signatures are a thing, you know."

His beard twitched. "I know, sassy girl, but this is a pretty big thing."

"I signed earlier this morning. The deal is done."

"Just like that?" Mom asked.

"Just like that."

"Well, tell us everything," Dad said, sitting back down.

So, I did. I was getting a nice little advance, but it was the knowledge I'd have a paperback in my hand, proof of my having accomplished that part of my dream within the year.

"A year? Why so long?" Dad asked.

I rolled my eyes. The old fart knew nothing about the publishing world. "The process is a long one—nothing I can do about it."

He studied me, having sat back, plate pushed aside, and arms crossed. "So, what will you do in the meantime?"

I shrugged and picked up my wine glass Mom had topped off to celebrate again. "Eventually, I'll sit down and plan out another series. Or standalone." I sipped and shrugged again. "Not really sure."

Dad glanced at Mom, and they shared one of their looks, the kind that escaped my brain's ability to understand, but one they seemed to read without issue.

"So, you're free for a time?" Dad finally looked my way.

I knew his tone, *that* look at least. "What did you have in mind?"

"Come fly with me."

I hadn't flown all summer. Hadn't gone beyond Dad and Mom's property in town, not to the store, not to Fairbanks to visit old friends from college, or even Kari when she'd invited me for a weekend getaway.

"Take a break," Dad insisted. "Come fly the skies with me like we used to do when you were a kid. I need some time with my little girl before you outgrow this house."

My damn heart melted, and I smiled. "That sounds like fun."

His eyes misted over. "It's a date, then. You're mine for the day—Saturday?"

"Sure."

He shared another smile with Mom, and I picked up my wine. "To getting back too normal—or a new one, at least," I said.

Both of them raised their glasses.

Dad winked at Mom and we clinked our goblets together.

"Something new," Dad agreed, his smirk tickling my curiosity.

"So how much of an advance did you get and when does your book release?" Mom asked, and I turned to her, more excited than I could remember.

Yes, my heart ached for Roan, I still missed him, dreamed of him, but I'd managed to move on. I wondered, though, if I hadn't fulfilled my dream, if I would have been able to let him go so easily.

I kidded myself, though.

That night, I allowed my brain to be fully consumed by memories—of my time at the homestead, of Roan. His low voice, his laughter, his touch. Arousal rose, choking off the heartache that returned full force, taking control of my brain, my body. Even the memory of fire, the fear of singeing heat couldn't overpower my need, my longing for him.

I brought myself to release, his name on my lips, and tears slid down my cheeks.

Sure, I'd accomplished the beginning of my dreams, but the high of that fact faded, leaving me just as heartbroken as before.

33

ANNIE

I sat bundled beside Dad in his Cessna, watching the mountains on the horizon—snowcapped and gorgeous. A pile of supplies lay in the cargo area, an order placed by a new homesteader.

We banked south, and I watched the familiar scenery below, the comfortable silence between Dad and me nice since I'd been plagued by all thoughts of Roan since finishing my books. Sleep didn't come easy, and I'd lost my appetite enough those ten pounds were on their way down the drain.

I needed to start a new book. Keep my mind focused on anything else but him.

But seeing the river in the distance brought back memories of our last time together while he'd burned with fever.

Did he miss me? Think of our time at all? Or was the fight for survival out in the wilderness enough to keep him occupied? The peace of Mother Nature enough to soothe whatever might linger?

He'd told me he loved me—then he left me behind.

My throat thickened, and I turned forward.

The land ahead dented my forehead with a frown, the sight of it too familiar for comfort.

"I don't want to see it, Dad," I whispered into the headset, and he heard, reaching for my hand.

"Do you trust me?"

I nodded, unable to trust my voice to rise above the race of my pulse. Swallowing to keep bile from rising, I forced myself to watch the land below, but rather than find the blackened earth my mind flashed in my mind, a dusting of fresh snow covered the land.

Pressing my forehead to the cold glass, I peered below, catching only hints of burned tree trunks jutting up from the pristine white.

The river lazed along, not yet frozen over.

"Look, Annie."

I took a deep breath to prepare myself for the burned cabin—and turned my attention toward where he gazed out the front of the plane.

A two-story cabin…fresh lumber. Smoke rising idly from a stone chimney…

"Dad?" I choked out, unable to believe a new home stood where our old cabin had burned to the ground. "Y-you rebuilt it?"

"Roan did—for you."

A sob ripped from my chest, and I clamped my hands over my mouth, attempting and failing to hold my emotions inside.

Dad buzzed the clearing, and when he banked, bringing us in line with the river to land, Roan stood on the stoop. At least I expected it was him—my eyes were too damn hazed up by tears.

The pull of the water on the pontoons jerked me forward,

and I stayed leaned that way, fighting to focus on the man striding down the snow-covered path on our left.

"Daddy," I whispered, laughing through my tears.

"Yeah, baby girl?"

"What did you do?"

"Sold the homestead to a young man hell bent on blazing his own future in the wilderness."

I laughed again, swiping at my tears as he pulled up onto the log ramp.

The second the engine shut off, I tore off my headset, unhooked my seatbelt, and hopped out onto shaky legs.

Roan stood onshore, hands fisted at his sides, broad shoulders covered by a thick, red flannel.

Our gazes collided, and more tears fell, but he held still as though frozen. Unsure what to say, what to do—same as the night I'd burned my hand. "Roan."

My whisper full of longing brought life to his eyes, and he strode straight into the damn water. I jumped into his arms, my legs going around his waist as our mouths crushed together.

Warm, delicious lips…tickling whiskers…hard torso and strong hands beneath my backside…

Home.

The saltiness of my tears couldn't ruin the taste of his mouth, and he drank down my cries, squeezing me tight.

"Stay with me," he rumbled against my lips, his forehead tipping against mine.

A command, but the tone begged, revealed a man in desperate need of me. An addition to my world, not a man attempting to morph me into his.

I grasped his whiskered cheeks in my hands and pulled back to peer into his gorgeous green eyes. Wet with tears, full of emotion, his gaze raised my arousal to breath-stealing heights.

"Since you asked so nicely," I sassed, my tone mostly air.

Roan narrowed his gaze and squeezed my ass until I yelped. "Don't ever change, my Annie girl."

"Not a chance in hell."

34

ROAN

I clutched Annie's hand, studying her profile as her dad lifted into the sky. No more tears tracked her pink cheeks, and the smile plumping them, had kept my dick stiff in my pants from the second I saw she'd flown out with Brock like we'd planned, like I'd hoped she would do.

He'd planned to surprise her—and hell, had he ever.

She'd sobbed and continued crying, clinging to my arm like Ma did to Pa, while I showed her the house her father, Pa, and even my sisters had helped build.

Brock had used a helicopter to fly in the lumber since everything lay ruined around us. He'd also bought us a 4-wheeler which Annie squealed over, solar panels with enough battery packs to keep the updated house running fully operational for days in bad weather.

I'd emptied my bank account, giving him every penny I had, and he held the note for the rest of the mortgage. A huge risk, knowing I would have to travel quite a ways to hunt for pelts, but he'd also gifted us a snowmobile for winter travel to check lines. I hoped spring would bring gold from the river's shores since Brock hadn't ever panned, too.

He'd helped us carry all the supplies to the new cabin—and Annie's things her mother had secretly packed up for her.

Annie had called her Mom from the new sat phone her dad handed her, and her tears of thankfulness and sass at being lied to about her little day trip, kept me grinning.

The grin faded as Brock disappeared into the horizon and Annie finally turned toward me, wrapping her arms around my waist, and tipping her head back to peer up at me.

"You love me," she murmured, a soft smile on her lips.

"So much it hurts."

"You want to fuck me." Her smile turned into a sassy smirk.

I pressed my aching dick against her belly. "So much it hurts," I growled.

She giggled as I yanked her up into my arms and spun, steady strides taking us up the path to our new home.

Home.

My throat tightened as I took in the amazing two-story lumber home Brock had insisted on. Fully insulated with a point well running up from the river, our home ensured my woman would live as close to a lavish lifestyle in the wilderness as possible.

Boxes stacked against the wall just inside the front door, but I ignored them, striding right up the open stairwell to the single room above, the heat of the wood stove rising to keep it warm as could be.

Too warm, I realized as I set Annie to her feet, a rush of heat over knowing I'd be sinking balls deep into her tight clutches in a matter of minutes.

I tore my flannel off without unbuttoning it all the way. Hopped on one foot while rushing to get my damn boots off.

Annie laughed and stood hands on hips, watching me, dark eyes flashing with amusement and lust.

I stripped down to nothing but skin, grabbed the base of my leaking dick to keep from blowing before it even got a lick of her wetness around its head.

She peered at my throbbing length, pupils damn near making her eyes appear black, her face flushed.

"Take off your clothes for me, Annie girl," I rasped, my voice rumbling.

"The python looks like it's ready to bite," she whispered, pulling off her sweatshirt.

My lips twitched, but I needed to fuck more than I needed to smile. "Hurry."

"Awfully bossy." She tossed her shoes aside and shoved down her thick leggings.

"You fuckin' love it—now hurry up before I shoot all over our bedroom floor."

She finally tore her focus off my dick and looked up at me through her lashes while kicking off her pants and panties. "Our bedroom."

"Our house. Our bed," I said through grit teeth, squeezing up along my length and staring at the hair between her thighs.

"Pull down on your sack."

"Huh?"

Annie stepped close and grasped my balls, gently tugging them away from my body.

"Fuckin' hell," I groaned, but the need to blow lessened.

"There." She smiled up at me and reached to unclasp her bra, leaving her in nothing but gorgeous, pale skin.

"Let me look at you…" My hand took to stroking in slow, long glides along my length, pre-cum dripping and slickening me up for her tight sheath. "Fucking beautiful—perfect, Annie. I can't wait to be inside you."

She backed up, her sassy smirk and quirking finger beckoning me forward like a damn leash—I stalked after her without thought. The foot of our bed hit the back of her knees, and she sat back, scooting her lush ass back until she settled in the center.

Eyes locked, I crawled after her, headed right for her spread thighs, sliding the tip of my dick up through her creamy slit—and sank in with one slow push, moving forward until she laid back, and I covered her body.

"Roan," she groaned, her legs wrapping around my ass, her fingernails going straight for the tensed muscles along my spine.

I held still—drank in her sweet breath, my dick throbbing and loving her wet heat clamped tight around me.

"You're staying the winter," I told her between grit teeth while pulling out until just the head of me felt the squeeze of her silken pussy.

"I'm staying for the rest of my life."

My grin took over. "So, you won't mind if I keep this one short and sweet?"

Annie narrowed her gaze and dug her fingernails in a little bit sharper. "I don't want sweet."

I thrust forward, jabbing as deep as I could go.

"Oh shit!" She gasped and blinked, and I ground against her clit with my pelvis.

"You want a good, hard fuck," I said, repeating the thrust. "You want me to fill you with my cum until it's leaking out of your tight, little hole."

"Yes." Her back arched, and I gave her what she wanted.

Hard. Deep. Rough.

And too fuckin' fast.

At least I managed to hold off until she cried out my name, her pussy creaming around my dick.

I might have pulled out quicker than my body wanted, too.

I definitely shoved my dripping seed back inside her body with my fingers.

My dick didn't go slack, so I sank back in and gave her slow and sweet, the mess we'd made on our sheets bringing the need to do laundry the next day.

But we would do the chore together. Me and my sweet Annie.

"You're mine," I murmured against her sweaty neck a long time later as one last shudder let a droplet or two of cum out of my dick against her womb.

"You know," she said, sliding her hands down my back and sighing, "you're the only man I don't mind bossing me around."

"Get used to it." I pushed up to plank over her, grinding my hips against her—but my dick had spent itself.

Her smile faded as she brushed hair off my sweaty brow.

I turned my face to kiss her scarred palm. "I love you, Annie."

She pulled me down and held my face, brushing her lips over mine. Better than our first kiss, the one I'd stolen, the one that had led to pain—but had brought us back together. Annie didn't need to reply.

Her kiss, freely given, told me all I needed to know.

35

BROCK

TWO YEARS LATER...

The unmistakable cry of a newborn baby jerked my eyes open, and I peered into the dimness, making out the fact I slept in a tent.

Annie.

Baby.

I reached to my side to find the other half of our blow-up mattress empty and cold. Jessie must have already gone in.

The cry came again—healthy and loud—and I grinned, a chuckle bubbling up inside me. Sitting on the mattress's edge, I grabbed my boots and shoved my feet in, not even bothering to take the time to lace them up.

My baby girl had her baby girl...

I unzipped the tent and stepped into the Alaskan night, the warmth of the night and the sun's refusal to fully rest making it easy to see across the green landscape. The tent a dozen or so feet away unzipped, and Flynn stepped out, one boot on, one dangling from his hand.

We shared a grin, and he hopped around, slipping his other boot on, while I started toward the brightly lit house. Soft, yellow light shone from the house's four windows.

The cry came again, and I took off, still smiling like a damn idiot. A healthy wail like that, the determined, lusty continuation of screams, meant my poor Annie would have her hands full.

I pushed through the front door and pulled up short as Jessie came down the stairs. Wisps of blonde hair had come loose from the braid down her back, and her pink cheeks and shining blue eyes stole my breath. Blew away my damn mind like a hurricane, same as the first time I'd laid eyes on her.

Energy to light a goddamn city burst inside me, and she launched herself into my arms, laughing. "Our poor daughter."

"She do a good job like you said she would?"

"Damn right."

"Everyone's okay?" I asked, moving into the cabin so Flynn could get around me.

"Perfect. The little stinker is sassy as hell already."

"I can tell." I squeezed the love of my life tight and set her back down as the wailing continued overhead. "Am I allowed up there yet?"

"Go on, Grandpa." Jessie swatted my ass, and I shot her a glare promising I'd give it right back if she weren't careful.

She tipped up an eyebrow as though egging me on.

"Later," I promised her.

Flynn took my wife's suggestion to go on as permission, too, and beat me to the stairs.

We tried to tiptoe, but in boots and excitement, we didn't do too good of a job.

My baby girl lounged in her bed against a pile of pillows, Kari, who'd come out to see her through the birth, fussing on one side. Roan sat on the other—and he held a little shrieking bundle.

"Give her over," Saige told him, holding out her arms.

Roan stared at the red face, seemingly baffled and at wit's end while doing as his ma told him. Blinking like an owl as Saige moved off, he sagged as though in relief.

That boy doesn't have a clue. I held in my chuckle, empathy rising inside me from knowing all-too well what raising a girl will do to a man.

Saige hunched around the tiny bundle, swaying with old-as-time instincts, a soft melody humming beneath her breath.

Sassy Squirt shut up in a matter of seconds.

"Saige," Flynn murmured at his wife, and I glanced over to find his eyes welled with tears. They shared a private, silent moment, and she smiled, winked, and went back to singing the old Irish ballad I recognized from an Alison Krauss remake. Something about a lover being mistaken for a swan and shot—morbid, but the squalling stopped, so I didn't complain.

"How's my baby girl?" I asked, moving around Flynn to check on Annie for myself since I expected Saige wouldn't be giving up her first grandchild anytime soon.

"Good, Dad. Exhausted as hell, but good."

"You were made for pushing out babies," Kari mumbled, stepping back to give me room.

"Good." Roan found his voice—and his grin. "Because I'm going to swell your belly with at least ten more."

Annie backhanded him and laughed. "You can try, but I'm not doing *that* again anytime soon."

Roan leaned down to kiss her, his lips lingering on hers. "You were amazing. I've never seen anything so damn beautiful. So strong. Love you so much."

"Love you more," she whispered, the love in her eyes the kind I saw in my wife's every damn day.

I waited for their moment to end before tugging on one of my daughter's braids.

She smiled up at me, the exhaustion evident in her face.

"Didn't get a chance to tell you last night when we flew in, but you hit the New York Times Bestseller list—for the fifth time in a row. Damn proud of you for crushing your dreams, little girl." I tugged her hair again.

Annie let out a heavy exhale and sank back, her smile soft, her gaze trailing after Saige as she continued to hum, Flynn poking at the bundle from over her shoulder. "I thought I knew what living is…what *love* is."

I grasped her hand and squeezed.

She turned toward me, tears in her eyes. "I love you, Daddy. Now more than ever."

Cupping her cheek, I leaned in to kiss her forehead. "Love you, too, little girl."

"I never thought I would find what you and Mom have, but Roan…" She let out another sigh, and my heart swelled knowing my little girl's was filled up to bursting like mine had.

Jessie arrived at the top of the stairs with a pitcher of water, and I moved out of her way so she could refill Annie's glass on the bed stand.

Stepping back, I gazed around the room, thinking over the highlights of my years in Alaska— and counting my blessings.

Guilt and secrets lay deep inside some of us, I knew, eyeing Flynn and Saige enraptured with their granddaughter my hands itched to hold, but old regrets and soothed-over pain, too.

Life at its finest.

Roan kissed my daughter's forehead like I had done, and Jessie tucked herself against my side.

Neither of us spoke, but we didn't need to.

Happiness flooded the room, found through heartache and tribulation, and while the wilderness hadn't always been kind to our families, Mother Nature allowed fate to steer us in the best way possible— to love.

THE END

———

ABOUT THE AUTHOR

Lynn Burke is an international bestselling and award-winning author. A stay-at-home mom, she's a lover of coffee and vino, and with three spawn and two fur babies underfoot, noise levels dictate the daily switch-over time. In her few quiet 'me' moments, she can be found hunched over her Mac, trying to type as fast as her muse spews hot stories.

You can find more about Lynn at her website: www.authorlynnburke.com

ALSO BY LYNN BURKE

Abel's Obsession

Divulging Secrets

Healing Storms

In Between

Reluctant Lumberjack

Resisting his Mate

The Playboy Bachelor

Billion Dollar Love Anthology

Blood Born Series

Bonds of Worship Series

Dark Leopards MC

Darkest Desires Series

Devil's Outlaws MC

Elite Escort Series

Fallen Gliders MC

Forbidden Obsession Duet

Found by Fate Series

Midnight Sun Series

Missing Link Series

Risso Family Series

Sandy Ridge Series

Vicious Vipers MC

www.ingramcontent.com/pod-product-compliance
Lightning Source LLC
Chambersburg PA
CBHW071303190726
48292CB00007B/2665